Vampire
Vacation

Vampire Vacation

Thomas McKean

AN AVON CAMELOT BOOK

for RUTH PITTER

VAMPIRE VACATION is an original publication of Avon Books.
This work has never before appeared in book form.

AVON BOOKS
A division of
The Hearst Corporation
105 Madison Avenue
New York, New York 10016

Text and illustrations copyright © 1986 by Thomas McKean
Published by arrangement with the author
Library of Congress Catalog Card Number: 85-48073
ISBN: 0-380-89808-X
R|L: 6.1

Library of Congress Cataloging in Publication Data

McKean, Thomas.
  Vampire vacation.

  (Avon Camelot book)
  Summary: The apparent reappearance of a legendary vampire threatens to ruin
business at a health resort unless three visiting children can solve the mystery.
  [1. Vampires—Fiction. 2. Mystery and detective stories]
  I. Title.
PZ7.M478656Vam   1986   [Fic]   85-48073

First Camelot Printing, March 1986

Printed in the U. S. A.

OPM   10   9   8   7   6

Contents

The Silo

Main Barn

Creamery

The Bush

The Garden

Long Grass

Main Paddock

Farm Drive

Open Area

Map of...

HIDDEN MOUNTAIN

HEALTH HOTEL

...kersville →

Thomas McK...

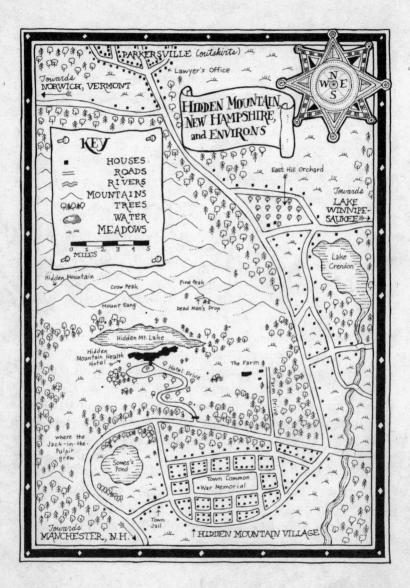

Chapter One

Trapped in a Tree

The screams started at two in the morning. They made you shiver, even under the covers of a warm bed. Loud and piercing, they echoed from the hills, lasting a good five minutes. Soft, then louder, anguished and horrible, they shattered the quiet of the countryside.

"Christopher Columbus!" cried Beth, leaping from her bed. "What on earth is going on around here?" Running to her brothers' room, she found Leo with his snub nose pressed up against the window. He was doing his best not to look scared as the unearthly screams continued.

"I—I've never heard anything like them," said Beth as she joined Leo by the window.

Turning away from the darkness outside, Leo asked, "What could be making them?"

"Beats me," replied Beth as the screams started subsiding.

"It sounds like something being killed—" began Leo, when Aunt Henrietta padded into the room. With her hair in curlers, green skin cream plastered all over her face, and the weird neck device she wore to bed to avoid straining her neck when she was asleep still in place, Aunt Henrietta was nearly something to scream about herself.

"This shall surely give me a migraine, not to mention insomnia," she announced. "And I shouldn't be surprised if it makes young Teasdale shockingly ill! How is my nephew?"

Looking on the bed, we saw our brother. He was wearing his purple silk pajamas and had fainted. No one was alarmed by this—Teasdale always faints when he's frightened.

1

"He does not know his luck," Aunt Henrietta told us. "Perhaps he shall go directly into slumber, and not suffer the whole night awake, as I undoubtedly shall!" She then stumbled wearily from the room.

"What a weirdo!" commented Beth. "Here it is, two A.M., and she doesn't even tell us to get to bed, the way our dad would!"

"Yeah," agreed Leo. "I can't figure her out! And I can't figure out those screams either!"

"Neither can I—but we'll get to the bottom of them, or my name isn't Beth Smith!"

A moan from the bed interrupted our discussion. Teasdale had de-fainted, and in a quavering voice he asked:

> "Did I hear a gruesome scream,
> Or was it just a dreadful dream?"

"Don't worry about it, Teas," answered Beth gently. "Just go to sleep, and Leo and I will tell you all about it in the morning."

So Teasdale went off to sleep. We were glad he was able to, but it did seem a little unfair. After all, we wouldn't have been where we were if it hadn't been for Teasdale.

I can see I'd better explain.

Normally, we live in Hartsdale, New York, with our dad, a lawyer named James Smith. There are three kids in the family: Beth, Teasdale, and Leo. Beth is the eldest and she's a great athlete; Teasdale's the middle and he's a poet (in fact, as you probably noticed he even talks in rhyme); and Leo's the youngest and an expert on UFOs and things like that. (By the way, one of us is telling this story—but I'm not going to say which. You'll have to guess.)

One day Teasdale saw what he claimed was a bluebird, although Beth thought it looked more like a blue jay. In-spired by his bluebird—though Beth still says it was a blue

2

jay—Teasdale decided to write an epic poem: "The Lovely Life of a Very Blue Bluebird." He also decided he would do research for this poem and really learn all about bluebirds. We all thought this meant going to the library and reading a lot of encyclopedias, which is what any normal person would have done. But not Teasdale.

Instead he decided he would learn firsthand what it felt like to sit in a tree all night. So without telling anyone, Teasdale sneaked out of his bedroom around ten o'clock, wearing only his pajama bottoms and carrying a long piece of rope. Halfway down our driveway he found a large maple which he proceeded to climb, even though he is truly afraid of heights. At exactly four and a half feet above ground level, Teasdale found a sturdy branch on which to spend the night. In case he fell asleep later on, Teasdale tied himself to the tree with the rope he had brought. And like a lot of people, he was much better at tying knots than untying them. I guess it wasn't his fault that it suddenly started to rain buckets of water and continued to do so all night. And I suppose it wasn't his fault either that he couldn't untie the knots in the dark when the rope got all wet and his hands were frozen.

To put it simply, Teasdale ended up learning a lot more about what it's like to be a bird in a tree than he'd bargained for.

It wasn't until breakfast the next morning that we noticed Teasdale was missing. At first we thought he'd gone to the library to take out some books about bluebirds but then we remembered it was Sunday and the library was closed—and even Teasdale knows the days of the week. So we began a search party. Leo was convinced he'd been kidnapped by Martians, especially when he saw the burned patch on the lawn near the house—but then Beth reminded him about the little trouble we'd had making the fire to cook marshmallows that we'd decided not to tell our dad about.

3

It was our dad who heard faint cries for help amid a lot of sneezing and coughing and thus was the one to find poor Teasdale. Beth would have been the one to find him except she happened to look in all the places where Teasdale wasn't.

Teasdale was already so ill from his night trapped in a tree that our dad didn't even get mad at him. Instead he got mad at us for not taking better care of our brother, which I thought was pretty unfair. We take very good care of Teasdale. Our dad also called the doctor. He showed up quickly, and said that though Teasdale had caught a somewhat severe cold, it wasn't pneumonia, or anything like that.

Since Teasdale is the kind of person who can catch a cold just thinking about winter, it wasn't too surprising that he'd get one from a night out in the rain. But we were a bit surprised to hear the doctor say that Teasdale wasn't very sturdy for a ten-year-old, and needed a bit of building up.

So while Teasdale was upstairs, blowing his nose and writing his will in rhyming couplets, our dad called our granny to ask her advice. We happened to be listening in on one of the extension phones, so we heard the entire conversation.

"So young Teasdale is not in the pink of health?" our granny remarked. "How distressing."

"Yes," sighed our dad, "and I don't know what to do about it. I'm right in the middle of an important case, so I can't take the kids anywhere, and I know you're busy now yourself . . ."

"I have it!" exclaimed our granny. "I know just the place: Hidden Mountain Health Hotel in New Hampshire! It's a large, old-fashioned sort of hotel that would be perfect. They grow all their own vegetables and produce all their own dairy products. And—"

"I know it well," interrupted our dad. "Remember, Elinor

4

and I went there for our honeymoon—she loved out-of-the-way places."

"Of course," our granny said; "I should have remembered . . . But if Teasdale goes, who shall take care of him?"

"Henrietta!" our dad answered. "My sister is the world's most accomplished hypochondriac—she'd love an expense-paid trip to a health resort! Of course, she's not the best companion for a ten-year-old, but I can send Beth and Leo along to keep Teasdale company!"

So it was decided. We three kids were pretty excited to go, even if we had to go with Aunt Henrietta. It was special, too, to be going to a place our mom had loved. Since our mom died a few years ago, we all like doing things she liked or going places where she had been.

Two days later, we three kids were put on an airplane to Boston where Aunt Henrietta lives. Our dad explained that Aunt Henrietta would meet us at the airport and drive us to Hidden Mountain Health Hotel: fresh air, good food, lovely countryside—and, it turned out, danger!

Aunt Henrietta and her Panhard

5

Chapter Two

Panhard to Paradise

Aunt Henrietta was there to meet us at the airport. Her yellow curls were disheveled and her eye makeup was smudged, as though she'd had it on rather too long. Beth thought Aunt Henrietta looked a lot older than her thirty-seven years. Our aunt also looked so exhausted we all felt she needed a trip to a health resort even more than Teasdale. It wasn't until later that we discovered that she'd arrived at the airport exactly twelve hours early! Only Aunt Henrietta could possibly imagine that when our dad said we'd be arriving at four thirty-six that he meant four thirty-six A.M.

But we were glad to see her anyway, even though she forgot which parking lot her car was in and it took us two hours to find it. Of course Teasdale was too weak to help us search, so he got to sit in the airport restaurant and drink orange juice and eat cinnnamon toast.

Finally we found Aunt Henrietta's car. It turned out to be something called a Panhard. A Panhard is a car they made in France around twenty years ago that was so funny-looking hardly anybody bought them and the company went out of business. Or so says Leo, who knows almost as much about cars as he knows about spaceships. And he knows as much about spaceships as any nine-year-old I've ever met.

The trip to New Hampshire was not exactly fun, especially for Beth, who had to sit in the front seat. Sitting in the front seat when Aunt Henrietta is driving is like sitting in the front row at a horror movie. Aunt Henrietta is the kind of driver who closes her eyes when she's driving if

6

she doesn't like the scenery. She says looking at ugly things gives her bloodshot eyes.

Somehow we arrived in one piece at the entrance of the Hidden Mountain property, just as the sun was starting to set. Aunt Henrietta was so excited when she saw the sign saying Hidden Mountain that she drove right into it and knocked it over. But that was really our only mishap on the entire journey. Beth thinks that Aunt Henrietta must be a very lucky person. Beth also thought that she, Teasdale, and Leo must be very lucky people when she saw how beautiful Hidden Mountain Health Hotel was.

After you turn off the side road where the Hidden Mountain sign is (or was, until Aunt Henrietta came along), you drive through the huge entrance gate, past an adorable little gatehouse, and then a good two or three miles along a small, twisty road. At the end of this road stands the hotel. From the front it's white and tall and very long, with pointy red roofs and funny little turrets sticking out of them. You can tell at a glance that the building was built in segments, each at a different time, each a bit different. So it ends up looking a little like an enormous wedding cake lying on its side. Teasdale said it reminded him of a castle he'd visited in the Bavarian Alps—where I happen to know he's never been—and Leo said it didn't remind him of anything: He'd never seen a building quite like it. Aunt Henrietta didn't say anything at all—she was too busy sneezing. But she did gasp out—between small ladylike sneezes—that there must be ragweed somewhere within fifteen miles of the hotel, and here she was, without her allergy pills handy.

Aunt Henrietta stopped sneezing long enough to park the Panhard and make us promise not to tell anyone it was she who'd knocked over the Hidden Mountain sign. Luckily the parking lot at Hidden Mountain wasn't gigantic, so at least Henrietta wouldn't be able to lose her car quite so easily—

7

though I must say, after having spent a few hours in it, that if that car were mine, I would *want* to lose it!

With our aunt behind us, sneezing again and complaining about a seriously stubbed toe, we three kids entered the hotel's majestic front door. We raced past the reception desk where Beth caught a glimpse of a silvery-haired woman in her seventies, and then we dashed through about twelve immense old-fashioned lounges, all filled with old gigantic overstuffed chairs, understuffed birds and beavers in glass cases, huge fireplaces, huger chandeliers, faded Indian rugs, flowers in colorful Chinese-looking vases, shelves lined with leather-bound books, and a lot of rather old people sitting around playing cards and reading magazines.

Forgetting our manners, we all started to scream with excitement when we'd cleared the last lounge and ended up on a large balcony from which we got a view out behind the hotel. The balcony overlooked an enormous lake, beyond which were some rocky cliffs, beyond which were some quite impressive mountains. There were also a number of funny little houses and small towers scattered around in the hills, which Teasdale proclaimed must house Kings and Queens in secret exile from cruel Ogres and Despots.

Beth was just about to tell Teasdale how unlikely that was when Henrietta joined us.

"Just look to your right," she told us, "and you'll see the farm."

So we did and sure enough we could just make out through a lot of pine trees a large red barn with a tall silo, surrounded by fenced-in fields full of cows. Beyond a field which seemed to be for grazing, Beth saw a good-sized vegetable garden, but she didn't mention this out loud because she knows what Leo thinks of vegetables.

"Christopher Columbus!" said Beth. "This place really is beautiful!"

And it was: The warm glow of sunset poured down on

8

us as we stood on the old wooden balcony, admiring the dark blue-green of the lake, the fringe of pine trees, and the rocky hills leading up to dreamy blue mountains. It was one of those sights that help Beth understand why Teasdale wants to write poetry. Even Leo stood still long enough to really look at it carefully.

So we were stunned when Teasdale turned away from the view and said simply:

"Though this place looks like Paradise,
There's something here that isn't nice!"

Before Beth could ask Teasdale what he was talking about, she felt a hand on her shoulder and heard an old but strong voice say:

"Welcome to Hidden Mountain! It is such a pleasure to have children here! We do so welcome them!"

The voice belonged to Mrs. Bell, the proprietress of Hidden Mountain.

"Yes," she repeated, "children are so welcome here—you're just what this old place needs. I'm certainly sorry illness has brought you this time, but I'm sure the pleasure you'll have here will entice you to return time and again!"

After she'd finished this speech, Mrs. Bell leaned over and did the unspeakable: She kissed all three of us on both cheeks. There are few things Beth dislikes more than being kissed by grown-ups, and she knows Leo feels the same way. I'm embarrassed to tell you that Teasdale likes kissing grown-ups and has even been known to go up and kiss old ladies on the street he's never seen before, even though our dad says that's carrying a good thing too far.

The funny thing was that none of us minded being kissed by Mrs. Bell—we all had taken an immediate liking to her. Beth liked the sturdy way she walked, Leo liked her long white hair tied up in a bun, and Teasdale admired her clear

9

blue eyes. Only Aunt Henrietta said she was the kind of old lady she could do very well without, but Beth thought that might be because Mrs. Bell hadn't kissed her and she was feeling jealous.

"Yes," Mrs. Bell beamed. "I just know you'll have a wonderful stay, and in no time at all little Teasdale will be feeling up to snuff..." Here she paused a moment before continuing. "I just wish I could escort you to your rooms and personally help you settle in, but, um, you see, there's an awfully important board meeting coming up in just a few days and I—I have to go over some papers in preparation, and, uh, besides, something else has come up..."

Beth, who'd been watching Mrs. Bell closely as she'd been speaking, saw a brief but unmistakable look of worry cross the old lady's face as she mentioned the board meeting. Even Leo, who is not always the world's most observant kid, noticed it too. On the way to our rooms, after we'd said good-bye to Mrs. Bell, we talked about what it was that might be troubling her.

"Perhaps she has sinus trouble, as I do," suggested Henrietta. "Or perhaps her allergies have been acting up—and no one knows more than I do how debilitating these so-called minor illnesses can be."

"I know the reason for that look," began Teasdale. "She has surely misplaced her favorite poetry book."

"Maybe she's worried about Martian invaders landing on that gigantic balcony we were standing on," proposed Leo.

"Who knows," said Beth. "But I do know that nice old lady is worried about something—and I plan to find out what it is!"

"And I'll help," chimed in Leo. "That Mrs. Bell—she's as great as a granny!"

Beth then asked Teasdale what he'd meant about something at Hidden Mountain not being nice.

10

"I don't know; I can't explain," he responded. "It's a feeling that came but didn't remain."

Our rooms were great. We had a suite, with Teasdale and Leo sharing a large double, and Beth and Henrietta in small singles on the other side of a sitting room. All four rooms had balconies, and if you were brave you could climb over the railing and get from one balcony to the other without going into the room at all. Beth thought this would be an ideal arrangement if you were a burglar, but Aunt Henrietta said only a madman would risk life and limb climbing from one balcony to the next. The second Aunt Henrietta went off to unpack, Beth tried it, and it wasn't half as hard as Aunt Henrietta made it sound.

Aunt Henrietta said that since it had become so late, we would order a light dinner in our rooms. Aunt Henrietta claims that a heavy dinner soon before bed can damage the intestines.

Since Beth's and Leo's idea of unpacking is just opening a drawer and dumping everything in your suitcase into it we had some spare time before dinner came. Leaving Aunt Henrietta to carefully arrange her pill bottles in the medicine cabinet and Teasdale to put his poetry books on the shelf in alphabetical order, we quickly explored the hotel. We discovered it had over two hundred bedrooms, eight staircases, two elevators, three kitchens, and two dining rooms, and was built in the middle of almost two thousand acres. This last fact we learned from an old man sitting on a small balcony overlooking the parking lot.

"Look at all them shiny cars," he said as he rocked in a shaky-looking rocking chair. "They got two thousand acres to park them cars in, and they all choose the same little spot. Kinda makes you wonder, don't it?"

"Not really," replied Beth, who had decided this little man with the enormous bushy eyebrows, who was dressed

11

in an old red and black hunting jacket, and who was puffing away on a soggy cigar, was a bit around the bend.

"Well, you never know, do you . . ." said the man.

"I guess not," replied Beth as she gave Leo a kick and we started to leave.

"Good-bye," called the old man in a cracking voice. "Come back and see me when you can stay longer—I'm always here, except for when I'm not. And if you can't find me, just ask for Pops—Pops Simon, that's what they call me."

"OK, Pops," said Beth. "We'll remember."

"And bring that other brother of yours—looked like a bright one to me."

"I wonder how he knew about Teasdale," said Leo as we headed back to our rooms.

"He was probably sitting there and saw us come in," suggested Beth. "Now let's hurry back so we can eat!"

After dinner, we all settled in for the night. But, as you already know, nobody got a good night's sleep because of the screams. Leo said they sounded like something out of a science fiction movie. Beth was sure they were like nothing she'd ever heard. She was also nearly sure they came from the direction of the farm.

"But what on a farm could make that kind of noise?" wondered Leo.

"I wish I knew," answered Beth. "But tomorrow we'll find out!"

"How?" Leo asked.

"By exploring the farm for clues. And I bet you a dollar these screams are why Mrs. Bell was looking so worried! Now let's get some sleep so we're ready for action in the morning!"

Chapter Three

"COW" Commences

Aunt Henrietta refused to let us go to the farm before breakfast. "People who skip the day's first meal are prone to digestive disorders," she informed us.

And at breakfast she wouldn't let us talk about the screams. She said they'd given her an earache in her left ear, and talking about them would doubtless give her one in her right.

"Let us simply say it was the worst night of my life," she told us. She needn't have bothered adding that she'd hardly slept a wink—she looked it. There were rings under her eyes large enough to go around Saturn, and she could hardly keep awake.

At this moment Teasdale looked up from the poetry book he'd been reading—on the sly, even though our dad says no polite person reads at the table—and looked inquisitively around the large dining room.

"Hmmm . . ." he said. "You know, I've eaten breakfast in many different places, but never have I seen so many worried-looking faces." He then went back to the poetry book hidden in his lap, leaving Beth and Leo to think over what he'd said.

A quick look around the dining room confirmed Teasdale's statement: A good percentage of the diners looked not only as tired as Henrietta, but also really worried.

"It's those screams," whispered Beth to Leo. "They all heard them too—that's why they're worried!"

"Yeah," agreed Leo as he ate his pancakes.

"I believe I asked you not to dwell on that unpleasant topic," said Aunt Henrietta. "But no matter—I'm sorry, children, but I simply must go lie down for a while. Having a sleepless night leaves me prone to severe sinus attacks, and no one knows more about just how painful they can be than myself."

After Henrietta had gone we started making plans.

"Listen," said Beth, "it's up to us to get to the bottom of this! First we explore the farm, then we'll go around interviewing guests to see what extra information we can pick up. We'll form a detective team!"

"Great!" agreed Leo, and even Teasdale said he'd join us. And since Leo always likes to have secret names for everything, Teasdale thought for a second and then christened our investigatory team "COW"—Children Observing Worry—and also announced that our top-secret password would be "Moo"!

Little could he have known how prophetic a choice this was!

It was a fifteen-minute walk to the farm, and Teasdale kept saying he'd rather be back in the hotel room snoozing, the way Aunt Henrietta was.

"Forget about her," groaned Beth. "You'd think someone who slept as much as she does wouldn't be so tired all the time. It's good fresh air that'll make you healthy, not lying around all the time and taking allergy pills like old Henhead."

"You call this fresh air?" giggled Leo, wrinkling his nose as we approached the cow barn.

"Well, what do you expect a barn to smell like?" Beth replied.

The barn was gigantic—from one end you could barely see down to the other. The air was hazy with hay dust that whirled and danced in the morning light that came slanting through the windows. The only sounds came from the two long rows of cows, heads held secure between metal rods

14

as they ate their breakfasts. They certainly were noisy eat
ers—much worse than we are, no matter what our dad says

We had just decided there didn't seem to be any majo
clues lurking in the barn when a friendly voice interrupte(
our discussion.

"Sure are a lot of cows, eh?" it said, and we turned around
to see a tall suntanned man with blond hair like straw, brown
eyes, and a nice wide smile.

"I'm Bill," he said, "I work here on the farm. It's me
who's responsible for putting the milk on your table—not
to mention the ice cream! I bet the ice cream here's the best
you ever tasted," he added, giving Leo a pat on the back.

"We don't know yet," explained Leo. "We just got here
last night."

"Is that so?" said Bill. "Then how's about you telling me
who you are, and then I'll take you on a little tour of the
farm."

We introduced ourselves, and Bill took us on a tour that
lasted at least half an hour and ended up with Teasdale falling
in love.

Bill showed us the feeding room, explained how the metal
things worked, and then told us that usually the cows spent
the night in there, and slept standing up. He also showed
us the outdoor corrals and then the small stalls where the
cows with calves were kept and a big stall for the bull that
we must never go near. You can bet we kept our eyes open
for any kind of clues—but there was nothing unusual to be
seen. Finally he showed us a few more stalls kept especially
for sick, old, and injured cows.

It was in one of these that Teasdale fell in love.

"Who is this?" he asked, stopping dead in his tracks
outside a small stall near the end of the barn.

"That," answered Bill, "why, that's Rose—she's about
the oldest cow on the farm. She won't last too much longer."

Teasdale gazed a moment in silence at the hazel eyes with

15

their sad expression, and the brown and white body with its sagging back, and said:

"Don't ask me why, don't ask me how,
But I've fallen in love with Rose the cow!"

"Well I'll be goldarned!" chuckled Bill, who wasn't used to Teasdale's style of speaking. "If that don't beat all—the kid's fallen for a cow!"

So while Bill showed us the hayloft and the grain silo, Teasdale stayed by Rose's side in the quiet barn, probably reciting poetry to her nonstop.

In the silo we met Frank, another farmhand who seemed almost as nice as Bill. He helped us climb the shaky ladder that went up the enormous silo and didn't get mad when by mistake Leo kicked down a shower of grain all over his curly brown hair.

"And you know," remarked Frank as we sat up in the silo, "there are lots of spooky legends about Hidden Mountain."

"Such as what?" Leo demanded.

"Well," Frank replied, "I'll tell you some other time . . . I, uh, don't think Mrs. Bell would like me telling you when you've just arrived!"

"At least tell us one thing," said Beth. "Do those screams have anything to do with the legends?"

"Let's hope not" was Frank's mysterious response.

When at last we returned to Teasdale we found him kicking the ground the way he does when he's upset about something.

At first Beth thought he'd had a lover's quarrel with Rose, but Teasdale explained that a mean and grumpy man had come from nowhere and yelled at him, saying that children shouldn't be alone in the barn because it wasn't safe and

16

their insurance didn't cover accidents to guests on farm property, and he didn't want to see Teasdale there again, or any of us kids, and so on and so forth.

Bill asked Teasdale to describe who it was who had been so rude, and when Teasdale said it had been a man in his late twenties with green eyes, shiny brown hair, and a strong build, Bill knew right away who it was.

"Jon," he told us. "One of the other farmhands. He and his brother were raised on a farm somewhere, so Jon thinks he knows everything!" Leo and Beth promptly decided we didn't like this Jon at all, even though we'd never met him.

After Bill and Frank left us, we did a bit more clue-searching on our own. The only unusual thing we found was near some pine trees, a little ways from one of the outdoor paddocks: This was a whole lot of footprints. It looked as though a few people had been walking around looking for something.

"This," announced Leo, "is very weird!"

"Why?" asked Beth.

"It reminds me of a science fiction film I saw," explained Leo. "You see, in the movie they found a lot of strange scratches in a place on their spaceship where nobody went. And that's how they knew the Martian invaders had boarded."

"So?"

"So, why should so many people be stomping around here, so far from anything? I can see footprints of at least three different kinds of shoes, here in the dirt. Somebody has to be up to something—I just know it!" Leo replied. "And who knows? Maybe it has something to do with those legends Frank was talking about."

"Makes sense, I guess," agreed Beth as we started back for the hotel. "As soon as we get to know Bill and Frank better, we'll make them tell us about those legends. Now let's get back in time for lunch, or Henhead will start worrying about our digestion!"

It turned out we had half an hour to kill before lunch.

"Let's check out the balcony," suggested Beth. "Maybe we can see something from up there."

On the way to the balcony, we passed the reception desk, where a lot of loud shouts and angry words commanded our attention. A moment later we were carefully concealed behind a large potted palm just a bit to the left of the desk.

"This is what I call perfect!" stated Leo. "These huge dumb old indoor trees are just made for spying!"

"Hush!" ordered Beth. "I want to hear what all the shouting is about!"

"You have a nerve calling this place a health hotel!" an irate man in his sixties was telling a tired desk clerk. "My wife and I drove all the way from Philadelphia two days ago for some peace and quiet!"

"But Hidden Mountain is the picture of peace and quiet," protested the clerk.

"Not in my book!" answered the angry guest. "My wife's doctor recommended a week away from the noise of the city—he said clean air and quiet countryside would do wonders for my wife's health. Well, we got the clean air, but not the quiet! We're checking out!"

The man then slammed his room keys down on the desk and hurried toward the front door, his wife struggling to catch up.

Charging out from behind the palm, Beth got to the front door at the same time as the man.

"Hold on a second!" Beth called out. "Why are you leaving?"

The man gave Beth an annoyed expression and then replied, "Why do you think? It's those screams. My wife can't sleep after she hears them and, frankly, neither can I!"

18

"It looks as though we're not the only ones who've heard those screams," reported Beth as she returned to the safety of the palm. "Let's hang around a little longer, just to see if any more people check out for the same reason."

We didn't have long to wait. Three and a half minutes later two elderly ladies, dressed in nice old-fashioned clothes, approached the desk and politely rang the bell that summoned the desk clerk.

"May I help you?" he asked.

"Yes," the stouter of the two ladies began. "We're so awfully sorry to trouble you, but my companion and I are compelled for urgent family reasons to leave two days early, so we would like to check out as of this afternoon. We trust there will be no difficulty in doing so."

"None at all," sighed the desk clerk and set to filling out the proper forms.

"See," said Leo, "they're not checking out because of the screams—they just have to go."

"Want to bet?" Beth replied. "Listen—those two are the kind of people who'd be polite in an earthquake! I bet they just made up all that stuff about family reasons so they wouldn't offend anyone . . ."

"Excuse me," said Beth a moment later in her politest voice.

"Yes?" replied the stout old lady.

"My name is Beth Smith and I'm doing a school assignment on, um, sleep habits in the country versus sleep habits, um, not in the country, and I'd like to ask you a few questions, if I may."

"Isn't summer an odd time to be doing a school assignment?" inquired the old lady.

"Oh," said Beth. "Um, it's, um, it's—I've got it! It's extra credit for next year! I'm starting early to get ahead!"

"How admirable!"

19

"Thank you," Beth replied. "Now, my first question is, how did you sleep last night?"

"Abominably!" the lady stated. "Now I'm afraid I must leave you. My companion and I have much to do by the one-thirty checkout time. Good day, young lady, and good luck with your schoolwork."

Being an amateur scientist, as well as having read over four hundred science fiction novels, Leo claimed that what the old lady had said about sleeping abominably didn't really prove very much.

"Maybe she always sleeps abominably," he suggested. "Maybe it has nothing to do with the screams."

"You've got a point," admitted Beth. "But there is someone who might tell us if the screams are really driving people away."

"Please tell me . . . who that might be," said Teasdale.

"Mrs. Bell," was Beth's reply. "First we'll just ask her how she slept—and then we'll get on to some serious questions!"

Mrs. Bell's office was located on the second floor, right above where all the big freezers were. When we entered she was busy reading through some complicated-looking papers which she covered up the second she saw we were there.

"Why . . . um, hello," she said. "If it isn't the Smiths—and all looking so well—even little Teasdale! What can I do for you this fine day?"

Beth gazed deep into Mrs. Bell's eyes, and it was clear to her that Mrs. Bell had something pretty important on her mind.

"Oh, nothing much," replied Beth nonchalantly. "We just wanted to say hi—"

"—and see how you slept last night," blurted out Leo, never one to be exactly subtle.

"How I slept . . ." began Mrs. Bell with a pleasant smile. "Why, just fine . . ." she started as the smile slipped from her lips and an odd expression took its place. "Well," she continued, "to tell the truth I've had better nights . . . but let's talk about brighter subjects!"

"Oh, we don't have to—we like depressing things," lied Beth. "Don't we, boys?"

"Roger!" agreed Leo.

"Right!" said Teasdale. "If you want to make us glad, then tell us things depressing and sad!"

"What delightful children you are," smiled Mrs. Bell, except it seemed to Beth a sad sort of smile. "You're just what we need at this old hotel of mine . . . and I guess I can confide in you . . . I wonder if you recall my mentioning an important board meeting that was coming up? Well, it's in just a few days, and I'm afraid they might decide to close the hotel!"

"Close the hotel?" we gasped. "But why?"

"It all boils down to a question of money," Mrs. Bell sighed. "You see, even though I own this place, certain decisions concerning its operation are controlled by the Board of Directors. And I'm afraid the hotel has been losing rather a lot of money recently. Last year it was all that rain, and this summer it's . . . it's . . . oh, I don't even know where to begin . . ."

"It has to do with those screams, doesn't it?" said Beth.

Mrs. Bell seemed to shudder. "You're right. I wasn't going to mention it in case you hadn't heard them yet. It's almost as if someone is trying to drive us out of business . . ."

"But who?" we wondered.

"I have my suspicions," replied Mrs. Bell slowly, "but it wouldn't be fair to point a finger until I have more proof

21

. . . and I haven't even mentioned the old legends about this place. They're . . . they're . . ."

"They're what?"

"They're— No, I'd rather not frighten you—and I know how sensitive Teasdale is . . ." muttered Mrs. Bell.

"Hmmm," mused Beth. "Frank wouldn't tell us either. But maybe things aren't as bad as they seem. Maybe the screams aren't bothering *that* many people."

"Possibly," answered Mrs. Bell, though she didn't look us in the face when she spoke. "I won't know for sure until I see exactly how many people have checked out early and how many people have canceled their reservations."

"Hmmm . . ." said Beth. "Maybe we can help out."

"But how?" wondered Mrs. Bell.

"By chatting with a few guests—though not in an obvious way, of course—and seeing what we can learn about the screams, and how people are reacting to them. Would that help?"

"Why bless your little heart," said Mrs. Bell. "I do believe that would help me out just fine!"

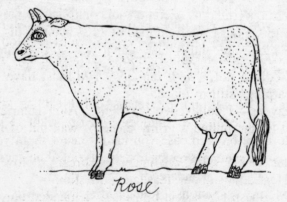

Rose

Chapter Four

"COW" Continues

We put off our interviewing until after lunch. Even Sherlock Holmes had to stop to eat sometimes.

Aunt Henrietta finished her morning nap in time to join us, though she still looked a wreck. She was busily sucking on some throat lozenges as Beth cautiously brought up the subject of the screams. Our aunt may be eccentric, but Beth has noticed she can be quite observant. So Beth figured even Henrietta might tell us something worth knowing—the only difficulty would be in getting her to talk about the screams. Thinking quickly, Beth came up with a good plan. The only hitch was that it involved Teasdale—and Beth didn't have the time to warn him.

"Aunt Henrietta," Beth began, "Teasdale has something he wants to ask you."

"I do?" said Teasdale, his eyebrows disappearing with surprise under his dark bangs.

"Yes, you do," continued Beth. Teasdale was still looking confused, so Beth said our secret password—"Moo."

"Moo?" repeated Aunt Henrietta. "Did you say 'moo'?"

"Of course not," Beth replied. "You must have one of your earplugs still in place."

"Heavens—I believe you're right," Aunt Henrietta answered as she pulled a grimy piece of wax out of her left ear.

"What luck!" said Beth under her breath. "Now listen, Aunt Henrietta—about Teasdale's question—"

"Why doesn't he ask it himself?" demanded our aunt.

"Um, because he's feeling shy today. Anyway, Teasdale

is writing a poem about those screams, and he can't think of what they remind him of. Do you have any ideas?"

"Well," sniffed Aunt Henrietta. "I'm sure I never told you, but shortly after my divorce I took a trip to Ireland, and I was staying in a small hotel in the country. At any rate, during the night, one of the sheep got loose and the poor thing was hit by a car. It was badly injured, and the sound it made until the vet could come was just like the screams we heard last night."

"Tell me what happened to the sheep before I start to weep," begged Teasdale.

"Luckily, the doctor was able to save its life," Aunt Henrietta informed us.

Even so, the story took away Teasdale's appetite.

"Finish your lunch, Teas," Beth told him. "Remember, you're here to get strong!"

"That was a pretty terrible story old Henhead told us at lunch," commented Leo afterward as we started off to do some interviewing. "Leave it to her to bring up something so awful!"

"Well, we did ask her," Beth countered. "And it was kind of helpful—I mean, now that I think about it, those screams do sound like an animal in pain."

"Henhead's the pain, if you ask me," Leo replied.

"She sure can be," agreed Beth. "But then sometimes I remember all the rotten stuff that's happened to her. You know—her husband she adored so much just left her for no reason. Dad said it really broke her heart."

"Maybe," said Leo. "But it seems to me she's suffering more from heartburn than heartache!"

"You have a point there!" laughed Beth as we made our way up a stairway to one of the hotel's many wings.

* * *

24

We'd decided to investigate by conducting a survey about the quality of the food at Hidden Mountain. One thing I've learned is that people always love talking about food. Besides picking up information, conducting a survey is also a good way to meet a lot of people in a very short time. We met at least thirty-four people in the course of the afternoon, but I'm only going to tell you about three or four, and one of these you've heard about already. Beth and Leo did the investigating alone this time, as Teasdale was feeling fatigued, and had gone back to our suite with Henhead to take a nap.

The fifth door we knocked on was opened by a woman around forty years old, and so fat we wondered how she managed to get through it! She was very friendly, and invited us in to eat some cookies. Her name was Sofia Fillipelli, but all of her friends called her Filly. Because she looked a bit like a horse, we couldn't help but giggle.

"It *is* kind of a funny name," chuckled Mrs. Fillipelli in her loud deep voice, and gave one of her enormous legs a big slap. We soon learned that whenever Mrs. Fillipelli found anything the slightest bit amusing she'd give a noisy chuckle and slap her thigh. She was probably the most cheerful person we'd ever met. And she certainly was the fattest; she had more chins than we could count and her red dress looked like a tent. We liked her straight off and wished Teasdale and Henhead had been there with us; they both could have used meeting someone so exuberant.

"How do I like the food?" repeated Mrs. Fillipelli thoughtfully. She squinted her eyes for a moment so they disappeared into rolls of fat, then replied with a chuckle, "Great! Absolutely great! Greater than great!—except for one little thing: There isn't enough of it for the likes of me. Not by a long shot!" she added, slapping her thigh and then Leo's back.

She was awfully strong; her slap sent Leo flying across

25

the room. He said he didn't mind and that Mrs. Fillipelli should stop apologizing—flying across rooms was good practice for later, when he grew up and became an astronaut and would have to get used to being weightless.

This interested Mrs. Fillipelli greatly, and since Leo had told her sort of a secret, Mrs. Fillipelli said she'd tell us one. It turned out that since she often got hungry at night, she'd discovered a way to sneak into the kitchen after it closed and take food out of the freezer—mainly ice cream.

"It makes the best late-night snack," she informed us. She also invited us to meet her in the kitchen some night for an ice cream run.

"Sounds good," said Beth enthusiastically. "And, speaking of night," she went on, "by any chance have you heard some screams around two A.M.?"

"Heard 'em?" Mrs. Fillipelli bellowed. "Heard 'em! I bet my sister in Naples can hear 'em! It's no wonder the old couple next door checked out a week early!"

Mrs. Fillipelli said she was positive the hotel must be losing money. "But maybe," she added, "it won't turn out to be too bad—I mean, maybe the guests will get used to the screams. Let's just hope nothing else happens!"

"Such as?" we wondered.

"Who knows?" she replied. "But if there are screams in the night, then someone—or something—has to be making them. It only makes sense. And who can say what this someone or something might do next! It gives me gooseflesh to think about it! I might even check out early, but my husband Luigi is off on a business trip and won't be home for two weeks, and I sure hate being home without him— I get so lonesome I lose my appetite! And besides, the food here's too darn good to leave just on account of some screams!"

* * *

26

Anna was the next interviewee we found especially interesting. She was over seventy, with wavy gray hair, a large kindly face, and a shrewd expression. She was from the Bronx, she told us, and couldn't wait to get back there.

"A pleasant place this hotel is not!" she said. "Only because my children save and pinch their pennies to send me am I remaining here. If I left I would hurt their feelings. And my grandchildren too—they want me to have a good time. But how, I ask you, can anyone have a good time when some crazy fool is screaming when he should be asleep? When I was a girl in Russia I lived on a farm and never did I hear a noise like this! And they say the Bronx is crazy! They must never have been here! I count the days until my son comes to get me! May they pass quickly! Never again will I go on vacation—next time I stay home!"

She told us all about her grandchildren and how well they did in school, so we told her about Teasdale and how smart he was.

"Him I would like to meet," she said. Because Beth likes it when people say nice things about Teasdale, she gave Anna some of the cookies Mrs. Fillipelli had given us when we left her.

Before we said good-bye to Anna, we remembered to ask her about the food: She said it was good enough, but her mother had cooked better back in the old days. And she thought the screams sounded like the music one of her nephews made—the one who was in a rock band.

Mr. O'Hanrahan, our third interesting interviewee, didn't exactly give us a hero's welcome, but he seemed unwilling to let us leave—at least at first. He talked more than Anna, and even though he certainly was amusing, he wasn't half as nice.

"Couldn't you see I was busy working on an important act?" he asked us crossly as he opened the door. He looked around fifty years old and had a pot belly he tried to hold in.

I'm afraid Leo didn't help out any at this point. He thought Mr. O'Hanrahan had said "pact" and not "act," so he imagined Mr. O'Hanrahan must be a famous politician.

"Are you the Governor of New Hampshire?" he asked. "And do you have any top-level ultrasecret documents on UFOs on you?"

Mr. O'Hanrahan threw his hands up in the air. "Oh, the life of an artist!" he sighed to the ceiling. He then looked at us in disgust and said, "My dear children, I am Clancy O'Hanrahan. No doubt you've heard of me?"

"Not recently," murmured Beth, trying to be polite.

"Never, in fact," corrected Leo cheerfully. Leo still doesn't know when to keep his mouth shut. But then he's only nine, and our dad says people with red hair often have big mouths.

"I beg your pardon!" sniffed Mr. O'Hanrahan. *"I* am Clancy O'Hanrahan, world-renowned playwright."

Neither of us had ever heard of him, but at least Beth had the good sense to say, "Oh yes, Clancy O'Hanrahan— I've heard of you time and again!"

"You have?" gasped Leo. "I haven—" he started to say when a sharp kick from Beth silenced him.

Mr. O'Hanrahan would hardly listen to our questions. He brushed them aside the way Henhead brushes dust off tables, then launched into a reading of his new play.

"It's a mystery, and all about children," he confided. "No doubt you'll be fascinated."

Beth immediately decided nothing Mr. O'Hanrahan could write would fascinate her.

After nearly twenty minutes of reading aloud to us, Mr. O'Hanrahan had to stop to breathe or cough or something and Beth managed to interrupt and say:

"Um, excuse me, but I really don't think kids talk the way you have them talk. Not even Teasdale."

"Yeah!" agreed Leo. "Your characters sound more like Martians than kids!"

Mr. O'Hanrahan turned red then white then red again. For a moment we were scared he'd explode. "I beg your pardon," he said. "I don't see what two children could possibly know about writing a play. I'll have to ask you to leave. I must return to my act."

We weren't exactly sad to be asked to leave, although we never did get to learn what Mr. O'Hanrahan thought about the cuisine at Hidden Mountain. Leo, however, did manage to ask what he thought about the screams.

"They don't interest me in the slightest," he informed us. "I am too busy writing my mystery to think about nonsense like that!"

The last interesting person we interviewed was Pops Simon, and we didn't interview him on purpose. After we left Mr. O'Hanrahan we were laughing so hard we couldn't control ourselves, and we ducked onto Pops's balcony so Mr. O'Hanrahan wouldn't hear us laughing at him.

"Long time no see," he observed.

"Yeah," agreed Leo.

"Listen, Pops," said Beth, abandoning the pretense of asking about the hotel's food, "have you heard weird screams in the night?"

"Screams?" he pondered. "Well, let me put it this way: I have and I haven't."

And he would say no more.

We had to tell Mrs. Bell that it didn't look very promising. By luck we ran into her soon after we left Pops Simon, and she'd ushered us into an out-of-the-way lounge to hear what we'd discovered.

"I was afraid of that," she said softly. "Oh, what will I tell the Board of Directors? Even if they don't vote to close the hotel, they could decide that I haven't dealt with this problem well, and vote to replace me with someone else."

"Don't worry!" said Beth encouragingly. "We'll come along and say how great you are! It's not your fault about the screams!"

"How sweet of you to offer," purred Mrs. Bell. "But I'm afraid the meeting is closed except to the people involved. Anyway, it's held in the lawyer's office, in a town about thirty miles from here, called Parkersville."

"Oh," said Beth.

"And the meeting's in just a few days—and heaven knows what I can tell them. Guests are checking out early—I've been over the books—and all because of those screams. I just have to know what's really going on at the farm, to prove to the board that I can handle the situation."

"You may not know now," boasted Beth, "but you will soon!"

"Whatever do you mean?" Mrs. Bell inquired.

"I mean tomorrow we go to the farm again and investigate until we really find something! We were there before, but I don't think we tried hard enough. We'll go tomorrow and I bet we find evidence or my name isn't Smith! Right, Leo?"

"Roger!" replied Leo. "We're going to find out what's behind this or else!"

"Heavens to Betsy!" smiled Mrs. Bell. "I do believe you dear children will do just that!"

Teasdale was dubious about going back to the farm.

"But how can we go there to investigate?" he wondered. "We might be chased off by the man full of hate!"

"You mean Jon," considered Beth. "Hmmm—you're right; I'd forgotten about him. He told us never to come back—what if we run into him?"

"No trouble," announced Leo. "We just go there under protection, like some space explorers I read about in a book

30

I just finished. They went into forbidden territory but no one hurt them because they'd gotten protection from the Over-Lord."

"The Over-Who?" asked Beth.

"In this case Mrs. Bell," Leo explained. "We'll ask her tomorrow for a note giving us permission to go all around the farm. I bet she'll say yes. Then Jon can't do anything to us."

"Excellent!" cheered Beth.

"Yes," put in Teasdale, "even if the farm is thick with foes, I'll still get to see my cow-friend Rose!"

We also decided to set our alarms for two A.M. so we could be on our balcony and listening when the screams started.

"That way," said Beth, "we'll have a better idea exactly where to look for clues."

So after Henhead had gone to bed with twice as much cotton stuffed in her ears as usual, we set the alarm clock and opened all the windows wide, just in case the screams started early.

"This is one mystery that won't stay unsolved long," announced Beth as she turned out the light.

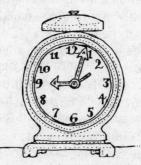

Chapter Five

Behind the Bush

It was a beautiful morning. The sun shone brightly through the windows, just as if it had nothing better to do. The birds were singing sweetly in the trees, the water was lapping merrily on the shores of the lake, the cows were mooing happily, and boy were Beth and Leo in a bad mood.

"Where is that alarm clock?" shouted Beth. "I thought I'd left it on the table. The dumb thing didn't go off, not to mention disappearing altogether! Where is it?"

"Aha!" exclaimed Leo. "I knew it—it's the only answer: Martians flew in and swiped it! They'd do anything to stop our investiga—"

"Can it with the Martian business," interrupted Beth, "and tell me why you have a piece of cotton in your left ear— you look like Henhead!"

Poking at his ear, Leo pulled out a piece of cotton. He then examined Beth carefully. "You've got one, too," he told her. "Check out your right ear."

"What the—" started Beth when a tired Aunt Henrietta padded in, still in her dressing gown and slippers and looking even worse than the day before. It was evident that she had either heard the screams again or had suffered another of her sinus attacks.

Aunt Henrietta made her way to the window, unlocked it, and opened it wide. "Perhaps a bit of fresh air will alleviate my excruciating headache," she sighed.

"Christopher Columbus!" exclaimed Beth. "Nothing worked! Who shut the windows? Who put cotton in our ears? Who—"

"I did, of course," replied Aunt Henrietta. "It seemed clear to me I must do all within my power to save you children from the health-threatening experience of hearing those frightful screams. Thus, after you were asleep, I shut the windows and placed cotton in your ears so you wouldn't hear a thing."

"Thanks for nothing," muttered Beth. "Where'd you put the alarm clock?"

"That I did not touch," our aunt responded. "Perhaps you misplaced it yourself."

"Of all the—" began Beth when a bedraggled Teasdale stumbled in from his and Leo's room. His dark hair was standing on end and he was clutching his stuffed elephant. He looked nearly as gruesome as when our dad had rescued him from the tree.

"Teasdale!" gasped Aunt Henrietta. "My poor child! Have you had a relapse?"

"It's not being ill that makes me feel so weary," he explained. "It's those screams that make me teary and bleary."

"You poor little thing!" Aunt Henrietta replied. "Too well do I know what you mean! You and I suffer from similarly acute senses of hearing! I shall get you some bufferin and a throat lozenge and a hot water bottle and some vitamins from the bathroom! I won't be but a second!"

We took advantage of Henhead's absence to grill Teasdale.

"What time did they start? Exactly where did they—" began Beth when an earsplitting shriek sounded from the bathroom. It was Henhead, who soon appeared in the doorway, pale and shaken.

"There is a madman loose in this hotel!" she announced. "I am going back to bed. I have developed the most shocking migraine. I simply must lie down."

"But what happened?" asked Beth and Leo in unison.

33

"Some vandal has put the alarm clock in the toilet," she responded, and was gone.

Don't ask me how we knew, but both Beth and Leo turned to our brother and said, "All right, Teasdale, tell us why."

Teasdale looked uncomfortable and then explained that he'd awoken around eleven-thirty, right in the middle of the most glorious dream—something to do with going back in time and meeting the poet Shelley and telling him not to go sailing. Teasdale told us he'd been so sure that later on in the course of the night's dreams he was going to meet Edna St. Vincent Millay, one of our mom's favorite poets, that he didn't want the alarm clock to disturb his slumber. So he decided to turn it off. Unfortunately, Teasdale is about as mechanically minded as a giraffe, and he couldn't figure out how to turn off the alarm. As Teasdale put it:

"Since my dream I knew the alarm clock would spoil it,
 I threw the alarm clock into the toilet."

We were about to throw Teasdale into the toilet when Beth remembered he was probably still a bit deranged from being ill. And she also remembered that just because Teasdale is a little different, that's no reason to be mean to him. So we decided to forgive him, on the condition that he tell us absolutely everything he could recall about the screams. Beth was also kind enough not to point out that despite his pitching the clock in the toilet, his sleep had been disturbed anyway.

All we really learned was that once again the screams started at two A.M. and came from the direction of the farm.

"So to the farm we go," announced Beth, "just the way we planned."

At breakfast Henhead revealed that she was going into town to buy some more aspirin and an extra package of cotton. After we walked her to the Panhard, we headed to Mrs. Bell's to get the note giving us permission to explore the farm. On the way, we passed one of the heads of the cleaning staff. She was talking to an employee, and we distinctly heard her say:

"There are a lot more people checking out today than we'd expected so don't dilly-dally! I want those rooms cleaned out pronto!"

Mrs. Bell turned out to be only too glad to give us the note we wanted. "In fact," she added, "you children can do me a favor. I have a note here for Bill—now, you're quite sure you, um, are going to the farm?"

"Quite sure, ma'am," replied Beth.

"How nice," responded Mrs. Bell without sounding as though she really meant it. "Now, where is that note? Oh dear, I can't quite put my finger on it. Could I trouble you to come back in ten minutes so I can write it again?"

"No sweat," said Beth. "See you then."

"Boy," continued Beth after we'd left Mrs. Bell, "she must really be upset about those screams—it's not like her to have mislaid something. She's the most organized person I've ever met."

"Yeah," said Leo. "She must have one big load on her mind."

"She's probably grieving 'cause so many folks are leaving" was Teasdale's opinion.

"Just one more thing," said Mrs. Bell in a low voice as she handed us both our permission letter and a note to Bill, "I'd like to ask you children to stay away from Jon, if at all possible."

"But why?" asked Beth.

"It's not a nice story," Mrs. Bell replied. "You see, my husband hired Jon about ten years ago, and I'm afraid he

35

wasn't always the best judge of character. Personally, I don't trust the man. But I kept Jon on, mostly out of respect for my late husband's wishes. But lately I have found Jon's attitude so negative, I had no choice but to give him notice."

"What did you say you gave him?" asked Leo.

"Notice, dear. That means I had to fire him, effective next fall. I thought it only fair to give him the summer to keep on working here, since he has been here so long. Though now I wish I hadn't, what with all my worries about that board meeting and everything."

"Don't worry about the board," Beth told her, "we won't let them close your hotel or replace you."

"Thank you, dear—I so appreciate your, um, concern. Now, I have a lot to do, and you have the farm to explore! Have a good time for me," added Mrs. Bell softly.

"I thought I told you to stay away from here!" an angry Jon bellowed at Teasdale when we arrived at the farm half an hour later. "And it went for your whole family, too!"

"Well," said Beth in a loud voice, "it just so happens we have a letter of permission from Mrs. Bell, *and* we're delivering a message to our friend Bill. So there!"

Jon shook his head, scowled, and stalked off.

"You'll stay away if you know what's good for you!" he called back over his shoulder.

"Thanks," said Bill. "The phone here at the farm is out of order and we're getting pretty sick of running back and forth to pick up messages. Thanks a bunch."

"Anytime," Beth replied. "Now we're off to explore. Hope you don't mind."

"Of course not," said Bill, "though there really isn't that much to see," he added quickly.

"We like looking at nothing," Beth explained. "Do you think Jon will keep on giving us a hard time?"

"I doubt it," Bill responded. "He's repainting the big silo, so he should be well out of your way the whole day. Now, before your exploring, why don't you drop by the milk vats—I'm pretty sure Frank'll be there and I bet he just might give you a swallow or two of fresh cream! I've got a chore or two to get done; maybe I'll see you later."

Jon was busy painting the silo. He must have started with the sun because he was already a third done. Even though he was pretty mean, we had to admire how quickly and well he painted. The brush seemed to fly across the old shingles and leave a perfect coat of rich red in its wake. He also was singing to himself as he painted, and he even had a good voice. I remember he was singing "Clementine," which happens to be one of Teasdale's favorite songs—I think mainly because it has such a sad ending.

Beth was just starting to think that such a good worker not to mention good singer couldn't be all bad when from halfway up the seventy-foot silo Jon caught a glimpse of us walking below and gave us a big scowl.

"Get outta here!" he shouted, and Beth changed her mind.

Frank wasn't in the creamery but luckily some Band-Aids were. We needed the Band-Aids because somehow Teasdale, in the midst of acre upon acre of farmland, managed to trip over an electric wire of some kind lying in the long grass and fall down and cut his arm.

"Couldn't you watch where you were going?" Leo wanted to know.

"I look where I go but alack and alas, I wasn't looking for a wire in the grass," explained Teasdale just as Frank entered the creamery.

"Hey, welcome back!" he said. "How's about a taste of some fresh cream?"

After we'd eaten more cream than was good for us, Frank

was nice enough to give us a little pitcher extra to bring back for Henhead. He also told us in secret that he had seen some early strawberries just a ways north of the larger of the two vegetable patches—which wasn't too far from where we'd seen all those footprints!

"They're right near the tomatoes," he whispered. "But don't tell anyone I told you!"

Even fresh strawberries couldn't tempt Teasdale into skipping his date with Rose.

"First I see my cow-friend Rose, she's sweeter than any strawberry that grows," he told us.

But Rose's pen was empty and there was nobody there to tell us where she was.

Teasdale looked mournful, then pronounced, "Perhaps Rose took a stroll to see . . . if she could catch a glimpse of me!"

Leo was convinced she'd been kidnapped by Martians, but to Beth it seemed far more likely she was out in a pasture somewhere enjoying the nice weather.

So we promised Teasdale we'd come back the next day on a special Rose-mission, and headed toward where we hoped the strawberry patch was, keeping our eyes open for clues as we went.

Weeding gardens, cutting grass, and picking vegetables are among the activities Teasdale refuses to do. He will, however, pick flowers, which explains why while Beth and Leo were laboriously bent over in the long grass gathering strawberries, Teasdale wandered a bit away from us in search of wild flowers. But he found a lot more than he was looking for.

"That sounded like Teasdale," remarked Beth a moment later.

38

"What did?" wondered Leo, who isn't always a good listener.

"That funny little scream from behind the bush. Listen—there it goes again."

Leo listened, shook his head, and observed, "No—it sounds more to me like some kind of bird or something."

"Perhaps you're right," began Beth when the sound of something falling through branches and hitting the ground issued from behind the bush. It was the familiar and unmistakable sound of Teasdale fainting.

Beth and Leo arrived behind the bush at the same time. They saw Teasdale lying face down in the long grass, his bunch of flowers scattered around him. And next to him, also lying in the long grass, and even more still than Teasdale, was Rose. And she was dead.

Usually when Teasdale faints, all it takes to revive him is a cup or two of ice water dumped on his head. But there wasn't exactly any ice water handy, and Teasdale seemed to be in a deeper faint than usual.

"Listen," said Beth, "you go find Bill—tell him we need help! I'll stay here with Teas, in case he de-faints. I don't want him to be all alone."

Leo dashed off to find help and, left behind, Beth couldn't help looking at Rose.

She wasn't a pretty sight. Beth is no doctor, so she couldn't tell how long Rose had been dead, but one thing was sure—she'd been dead awhile. She was already stiff. It also seemed clear how she had died—there were two awful marks in her neck, just as though she'd been bitten by some huge animal. Beth shuddered to think that some horrible mountain lion was loose in those parts when she thought of something odd—there were no claw marks anywhere on Rose, only the two teeth marks.

Leo and Bill puffed up at this moment.

"Oh my God!" gasped Bill. "What . . . what happened?"

"Something bit her," Beth informed him. "But worry about her later—we've got to get Teasdale back to the hotel!"

Fainted people are surprisingly heavy, even when they're as thin as Teasdale, but luckily Bill was strong, and before long we'd made it to his car.

We were trying to maneuver Teasdale into the back seat in a comfortable position when Jon appeared. Behind him we saw the silo nearly completely painted.

"I was just making a phone call . . ." he started and then noticed Teasdale. "What on earth happened to that kid?"

Beth hurriedly told Jon the story while Bill ran off to get his car keys.

Jon shook his head, looked a bit worried and then grumpy, and finally barked out, "I thought I told you to stay away from here! None of this would have happened if you'd listened to me!"

"Of all the—" began Beth when Bill appeared, and before she could finish her sentence, she, Teasdale, Leo, and Bill were on their way.

Henhead had just returned from town when we arrived, Bill carrying the still fainted Teasdale in his strong arms. He did look a bit dead, which I guess was why Henhead fainted too.

"Kinda runs in the family, eh?" was Bill's comment.

Henhead only had a brief faint, and when she revived and had heard the story, she dashed into the bathroom and reappeared with smelling salts which de-fainted Teasdale in two seconds flat.

But he was still so shaken Henhead insisted on calling the hotel doctor, who sent Teasdale to bed with a mild sedative and Henrietta to bed with a strong one. Mrs. Bell dropped by to express her concern and Bill left shortly after to see to things on the farm—and also to bury poor Rose.

"Listen, children," said Mrs. Bell in a low voice, "I know you've had a difficult afternoon, especially little Teasdale. But please—do me a favor, and don't spread around what you've seen today. I know there's a reason for it, um, somewhere—a wildcat, no doubt—and Bill and I are going to do all we can to, uh, find it. The reason, I mean."

"OK," said Beth slowly. "But it certainly was weird—those teeth marks, I mean. Really weird."

"I—I know," continued Mrs. Bell. "But trust me that I'll—I'll—I'll get to the bottom of it. You do trust me, don't you?"

"You bet!" we agreed, and then Leo blurted out, "But we don't trust that guy Jon! He was even mean when Teasdale fainted!"

"I'm not surprised to hear that," Mrs. Bell replied after a pause. "I can see now I'd better tell you everything. Perhaps you recall my mentioning that the Board of Directors might decide to close the hotel?"

"Yes," we said, "but we don't see how. You run Hidden Mountain, don't you?"

"I run it, of course I do . . . But you see it's the board that makes all the final decisions. And they have the right to close Hidden Mountain if it loses money two years running—and I have no say in the matter."

"But that's no fair!" protested Beth.

"It's just the way it is," replied Mrs. Bell. "Now, so far this year we've been losing a bit of money due to those screams—though not as much as we'd anticipated. It seems most of our guests are a pretty loyal bunch. But now, with this new, uh, development—why, mercy knows what will happen when the board meets!"

"Tell us," said Beth; "does this have anything to do with the legends you mentioned before?"

41

"Oh, Beth," sighed Mrs. Bell, "I just don't want to talk about it yet . . . I'm too worried already!"

"Oh, don't you worry," said Beth. "We're on your side! We'll make sure everything turns out all right!"

"What dear children you are," smiled Mrs. Bell, giving us each a kiss on her way out.

"You know as well as I do, don't you," said Leo after Mrs. Bell had gone, "that there aren't any wildcats in this part of New Hampshire."

"I know," said Beth quietly.

"And you know those two teeth marks you saw in Rose's neck?"

"Don't remind me," Beth sighed.

"You know what makes marks like that, don't you?"

"You've been reading too much science fiction type stuff!" said Beth angrily. "There's no such thing as a . . . as a . . . as a . . ."

"As a what?" Leo asked.

"I'd rather not say," Beth replied and left the room.

But Leo followed her. "We don't have to say it's that, yet," he went on.

"Of course we don't!" snapped Beth. "And anyway, for all we know, maybe it's just Jon, up to some weird trick to get back at Mrs. Bell for firing him!"

"Maybe," Leo said, "I don't know. But I do know one thing."

"Namely?"

"We have to keep on investigating. And I suggest we start by going to the farm at two in the morning when the screams start. Not that *I* have any doubt as to who—or should I say *what*—has been causing them!"

"We'll go tonight," said Beth grimly.

42

Chapter Six

A Terrifying Tale

Teasdale and Henhead were up and more or less recovered in time for us to have a late lunch together. It wasn't a big success. Henhead was in great distress; she claimed just hearing about the dead cow had given her an ear infection, and Teasdale wasn't too much better. His eyes were still red from crying over Rose.

Don't ask me how, but a lot of the guests seemed to have heard about Rose. We certainly didn't tell anybody, and neither did Henhead. I guess bad news just spreads itself. But everyone seemed affected by the morning's events.

Anna stopped by the table to see how we were doing and to meet Teasdale, and she forgot to mention her grandchildren; Pops Simon claimed there were no screams; and Mrs. Fillipelli even confided that her appetite was not all it had been. Only Mr. O'Hanrahan appeared oblivious to the turmoil around him. "Cow?" he asked. "What cow? What scream? I'm far too busy with my mystery to pay any mind to such childish doings!"

At least ten people came up to our table and wanted to know all about the bites on Rose's neck. We replied we'd rather not discuss it, the way Mrs. Bell had asked us to.

"You can't over up this kind of thing for long," one man remarked. "It's bound to hit the papers—people love this kind of story!"

"Some people might, but I do not," Henrietta interrupted. "Kindly leave us be so we may finish our lunch in peace. Your uncalled-for interruption is upsetting my young nephew Teasdale, not to mention myself."

"That's telling 'im!" cheered Beth as the man retreated. She likes it when Henhead shows a little spirit.

While Henhead was sloshing her tea against the back of her throat so the heat of the liquid would kill any stray germs (or so she claimed), we heard a loud crash from Teasdale's end of the table. Teasdale had dropped his teacup and was staring off across the dining room.

A moment later the explanation for Teasdale's action came walking over to our table. It was Jon and he looked grumpier than our dad did the time we thought his blue Mercedes would look more stylish if we painted it purple.

"I'm going to tell you one last time," he said, "and I'll tell you no more! Stay away from the farm!"

"Who was that rude young man?" Henhead inquired after Jon had left.

"So that's who he is!" she responded after we'd finished explaining. "I'd been wondering since this morning."

"Why?" Beth wanted to know.

"When I was in town this morning, doing my errands, I saw him outside the pharmacy. He was walking very fast and knocked over an elderly woman and he didn't even stop to see if she was all right."

"Sounds like Jon!" said Leo.

"Sure does," agreed Beth. "Except for one thing—Jon was painting the silo all morning. We saw him there. You must have seen someone who looked like him."

"Perhaps, dear," sighed Henrietta. "Though I could have sworn it was he. But most likely you're right. Those dreadful migraines I've developed as a result of worrying about those screams have no doubt affected my vision. I do believe I'll take a brief nap after lunch."

While Henhead napped, we did some investigating—at least Beth and Leo did. Teasdale decided to spend the afternoon writing a memorial ode to Rose. By the time we left him he had written as far as:

44

"Oh, my dear, my darling cow;
You're dead and we don't know how.
We went to see you in your pen
But you were not in. So then
"We went to the garden and I picked flow'rs
"And discovered you'd been dead for hours . . ."

There was a good deal more but I'll spare you the details.

"Why are we going back to the farm so soon?" wondered Leo as we approached the cow barn.

"It's just an idea I have," explained Beth. "I want to find out if those screams last night were poor Rose being killed."

"How can we find that out?" Leo asked.

"By seeing if somehow she could have gotten out of her pen and been on the loose last night around two A.M. And I want to ask Bill something—it makes sense that for every time there have been screams, a cow should be missing—if not dead. Right?"

"Not necessarily," answered Leo. "I mean the—the, uh, whatever it is that's doing all the killing—or at least the killing of Rose—uh, maybe it doesn't always kill cows. After all, the hotel guidebook said there were lots of deer in the woods around here."

"You've got a point," Beth replied. "All that science fiction you read sure seems to help you think! But I still think we should ask Bill if there are any other cows missing."

"Yeah," said Leo, "and we can also ask him about that legend Mrs. Bell keeps almost telling us about. I have a hunch I know what it is. I just wonder if Bill will tell us."

"Sure he will," said Beth. "He's our friend, isn't he?"

Bill wasn't in a good mood when we found him in the main barn. He was on the phone when we came in, and he didn't seem to be having a very nice conversation.

"No, Mrs. Bell," he was saying. "I don't know what he

45

was doing outside at that hour. Yes—I'll see it doesn't happen again." At this point he looked up and saw us. "Listen, Mrs. Bell," he said, "I've got company . . . Yeah, it's the kids . . . Right. Speak to you later."

"Hi, Bill," smiled Beth after Bill had hung up. "Having troubles?"

"Troubles!" mocked Bill. "Try disasters! First, the news gets out about how Rose was killed—I mean about those neck wounds, and people are checking out like rats leaving a sinking ship! And second, um . . ."

"Yes?"

"Uh, second, well, Mrs. Bell is mad as all heck!"

"Yeah," put in Leo. "We heard you talking to Mrs. Bell on the phone when we came in. All about someone being left out at the wrong time, or something. She must have been talking about Rose! Did you leave her out when she should have been in?"

"Well, Leo," said Bill, "you sure hit the nail on the head. It was me who left Rose outside last night—she's so old, I figured the fresh air might do her some good. I guess it didn't turn out that way. And besides—"

"Wait a second!" interrupted Beth. "You couldn't have been talking about Rose! You said 'he' and Rose was a 'she.' Right?"

"Right," replied Bill after a slight pause. "I wasn't sure which part of the conversation you'd overheard. Uh, you see Mrs. Bell is mad at me for two reasons—one is leaving Rose out and the other is, uh, because I let Frank off work early yesterday. Since we've cut back on the farm staff, Mrs. Bell gave strict orders that no one was to get any free time during work hours. She says it looks bad to the other staff. You know, to see someone having free time when they're usually working."

"Enough about Frank," burst out Leo. "Tell us if there are any other cows missing!"

46

"Missing cows?" asked Bill. "What are you talking about?"

"You don't have to act like everything's all right around us," Beth prompted. "Mrs. Bell's our friend and she knows we're kind of investigating."

"But about missing cows . . ." wondered Bill.

"Listen, Bill," continued Beth, "as I was telling Leo, it only makes sense that every time there've been screams, a cow would end up missing. Am I right?"

"Oh," said Bill, nodding his head. "I see what you mean." Bill then looked around him, just as though he were making sure no one else were listening. Then he scratched his cheek, brushed the blond hair off his forehead, and began. "OK, kids," he said, "since you've already guessed about the missing cows, I'm going to tell you something—but you have to promise me to keep it an absolute secret. And I mean absolute. Don't even tell your aunt!"

"Can we tell Teasdale?" demanded Beth.

"If you think he can take it," Bill replied. "Well—this may be hard to believe, but you've seen some evidence, so maybe it won't be all that difficult."

"Yeah, yeah," gasped Leo, "go on."

"Well, believe it or not, there's a legend about these hills that goes back a long ways—to the days of the French explorers at least. They say that's why that big ol' mountain just west of here's named what it is."

"What's its name?" Leo asked breathlessly.

"I know that," said Beth. "I remember seeing it on the hotel map. It's named Mount Sang. And that bumpy little pile of rocks at the top is called Crow Peak. What's so mysterious about that?"

"Do you speak French?" Bill inquired.

"We don't," replied Beth. "But Teasdale does."

"Well," said Bill slowly, "in French, the word 'sang' has one meaning—and it has nothing to do with singing. It means blood. And the word 'crow' is very much like the French word 'croix'—which means cross."

"So?" said Leo.

"So—the legend says that one Transylvanian Dracula escaped to America, and settled on Mount Sang. At least, it wasn't Mount Sang back then. It became known as that after a few murders supposedly took place there a long, long time ago."

"And Crow Peak?"

"They say it's called that because Dracula chased someone up there and was just about to kill him when whoever it was suddenly remembered that vampires are frightened of crucifixes—and produced a cross and was able to escape. So, I'm scared—scared that the vampire has come back to life!"

"I don't believe it!" stated Beth flatly.

"Neither did I till all this happened," said Bill. "I mean—who else could have killed Rose? And let me tell you—you've already guessed it, Beth, but she wasn't the first. There aren't any wildcats around here, and no bears either. And anyway, if it *had* been a wild animal, they'd have clawed the cows as well. And all there were were those awful teeth marks! We've lost at least seven cows—one for each night there've been those screams. And it's always happened at night—and everyone knows vampires like doing their dirty work after sundown!"

"I still don't believe it," said Beth.

"I believe it—I think," said Leo. "After all, there sure is a lot of evidence."

"You said it," agreed Bill, "too much evidence!"

After a bit more investigating turned up no more clues, we decided to go back to the hotel. Though before we did, we stopped in for another chat with Bill—Beth still had something on her mind.

48

"You know," Beth remarked, "that vampire—if there is a vampire—must be one pretty weird guy."

"Why?" wondered Bill.

"With all those healthy cows to kill, he chose an old sick one like Rose."

"People prefer old wine, don't they?" said Leo. "Maybe the vampire likes old cows."

"That's not funny," said Beth.

"Nothing about this is funny," commented Bill. "If these killings continue, and customers keep leaving, I'll lose my job! The board'll shut us down for sure! And it makes me feel extra bad to know that Mrs. Bell thinks a lot of it's my fault—that I haven't been keeping good enough watch at night—but a man has to sleep sometime! You see, I don't think Mrs. Bell really believes there's a vampire—she thinks there's a human being behind this, and that I should be able to stop him."

"Well," said Beth, "there's one way to find out if there *is* a vampire."

"What do you mean?" Leo demanded.

"What I mean is this—you and I are going to stand watch on this farm every night for a week! And if we find out there is a vampire, Mrs. Bell certainly can't blame Bill 'cause he was stealing cows—that wouldn't be fair! She'd know you'd done your best!"

"You kids are really brave," said Bill. "I don't know that I'd want to tangle with a vampire at two in the morning. But when you decide to stake out the farm, be sure to let me know. I wouldn't want to go shooting at any late-night intruders, and discover it's just you kids."

"You're telling me!" agreed Beth. "I'd say we had enough problems already, without being shot at!"

Chapter Seven

Death in the Darkness

Fifteen minutes after we left Bill, we had arrived at the front door of the main house, and were standing with Mrs. Bell as she was saying good-bye to some guests.

"You know," she said after they'd driven off, "the Mertons have spent every July for the past twenty-two years at Hidden Mountain. I never thought I'd live to see the day when they'd leave early. They said it was because Mrs. Merton's sister was ill, but I know that wasn't the real reason. It's those screams—and those awful rumors about Dra—about— Well, I don't even want to say the word. How can I operate a hotel which is supposed to be a health resort with all this going on? Not that I believe in Dra— in you-know-what, mind you. After all, I haven't been alive for seventy-two years for nothing. No, I feel there has to be another explanation. And I'm afraid part of the problem is Bill—much as I like him personally, I just don't understand how he can spend so much time at the farm and not have discovered any clues to what's going on."

"But Bill does a great job!" interjected Beth. "And he's a friend of ours, too!"

"Yes, dear," said Mrs. Bell. "I'm aware of your friendship with Bill. But my only chance of saving Hidden Mountain is to solve this mystery, and Bill hasn't been much help in putting an end to these stories about a vam—, a vam—, a you-know-what!"

"A vampire," Beth said for her. "Well, Mrs. Bell, that's exactly why Leo and I are here. We're going to find out what's going on at your farm tonight or our name isn't Smith!"

"Whatever do you mean?" asked Mrs. Bell softly.

"I mean Leo and I and maybe Teasdale will watch the farm starting tonight from around one o'clock till two or so. Kids do make good detectives—we're small enough to hide and we've sure got sharp eyes!"

"And ears," put in Leo.

"But my dear children, it might be dangerous! And whatever would your aunt say?"

"Henhead?" said Beth. "We just won't tell her. She's got enough to worry about with her sinuses and her migraines and all."

"I just don't know . . ." replied Mrs. Bell.

"Well I do," Beth told her. "We're going to do it no matter what! Right, Leo?"

"Roger!" Leo answered.

"You dear children are such a godsend! I'd be lost without you," purred Mrs. Bell. "Since I see I can't dissuade you, let me give you each a little something—just in case. Follow me . . ."

Walking back to our suite after our brief visit with Mrs. Bell to a storeroom near the kitchen, we each fondled the cloves of garlic Mrs. Bell had given us as protection. "Not that I really believe you'll need them," she assured us. "But better safe than sorry . . . I think it's the Greeks who believe garlic guards one against vampires!"

Mrs. Bell had managed to put the garlic on long pieces of string for us, so we could wear them around our necks, out of sight so interfering relatives wouldn't see them.

However, back in our rooms, Henrietta was in no mood to interfere.

"I've run out of allergy pills!" she informed us. "And today the pharmacy closes early! They refused to stay open just a bit later so I could drive in, even after I told them over the phone how badly I needed the pills! Some people

51

have no feeling for the sufferings of others! I'll just have to lie down, and hope I have no sudden attacks. I feel quite lost without them. And," she added, "to make matters worse, I do believe my sense of smell has been affected!"

"What do you mean?" asked Beth.

"I can hardly explain it," replied our aunt, "but all of a sudden I am smelling the most shocking odor of garlic! I really must go lie down," she concluded as she retreated into her room.

Teasdale's spirits were higher than Henhead's. He had finished his memorial ode to Rose, which he insisted on reading to us three times in a row. He would have read it four times, but Leo threatened to hide the special pen Teasdale writes all his poems with if he so much as whispered the poem again. Beth isn't so sure she likes poetry, but she likes doing things that make Teasdale happy.

Since you've already heard the beginning, I might as well tell you the end. The last few lines went like this:

> "So Rosie, good-bye, so Rosie farewell—
> I won't see you again on the farm.
> Too bad you had no lucky charm,
> But now in Cow-Heaven you dwell."

Beth wasn't positive what the lucky charm business was about but she didn't press for details. Teasdale doesn't take too kindly to criticism of his poetry.

So after we praised his memorial ode we immediately told him all we'd learned and of our intentions to watch the farm by night. To our surprise, Teasdale took the news without even growing pale, much less fainting, and to our further surprise wanted to come with us.

Teasdale then explained that he had suspected from the first moment he saw Rose's body that there was a vampire on the loose. He told us he'd begun writing a poem about Dracula which was one of his best.

"But," he said, "how can I describe Dracula to perfection unless I have the chance to make a personal inspection?"

Beth and Leo were a bit dubious about taking Teasdale along with us. It struck us that someone who faints at the drop of a feather wouldn't make the ideal comrade on a spy mission. But Teasdale vowed he wouldn't faint, and over an objection or two from Leo, was allowed to join us.

"But listen I pray," he continued, "I have something else to say."

"I'll only listen if you don't talk in rhyme," insisted Leo. "It's starting to make me dizzy!"

"All right," replied Teasdale. "I'll try. Remember we were calling our Investigating Team COW?"

"So?"

"Well," continued Teasdale, "hearing that word makes me sadder than anyone knows—you see it reminds me of my cow-friend, Rose."

"You're rhyming again," Leo told him.

"Sorry," said Teasdale. "So—would you mind if we changed the name of our team?"

"Of course not," Beth told him, "especially if the old name makes you feel sad. What should we be called?"

Teasdale thought a moment and then christened us "KIDS." "It stands for Kids Investigating Dracula Secretly," he informed us.

So while Leo made sure we all had enough dark clothes to wear that night, Beth dashed off to find Mrs. Bell and see if she had one more head of garlic she could give us . . .

Henhead was still feeling under the weather at dinner so she had room service bring in a salad and a cup of tea, and we got to go to the dining room ourselves.

"Poor old Henhead," remarked Beth as we walked down

53

the old-fashioned hallway, "she's sick more often than all the patients in a hospital put together. I wonder why our mom used to say Henhead was really a lot of fun to be with."

"Mom said that?" Leo exclaimed.

"She sure did," replied Beth. "But I guess no one's perfect—not even our mom."

"Oh no," said Teasdale, "there you're wrong: Our mom was perfect, and sweet as a song!"

Mrs. Fillipelli and Anna joined us for dinner. Anna spent a good part of the evening asking Teasdale what his grades in school were and comparing them to her grandchildren's. Mrs. Fillipelli spent dinner absolutely stuffing food into her mouth. Our tired waiter hardly got a chance to sit down the entire evening. Beth had never seen anyone eat so much at one time; Mrs. Fillipelli had obviously regained her appetite.

"It must be the scent of garlic I keep smelling," she explained. "Garlic always stimulates my appetite!"

Pops Simon wandered by after dinner. He told us he was chasing the bluebird of happiness and then added in a serious tone, "Did you know that seeing isn't always believing? Remember to think twice and look thrice! That's what my father said to me! Ev'ning, Mr. Teasdale!"

"He's as crazy as my Luigi's brother Antonio in Palermo," boomed Mrs. Fillipelli after Pops had gone.

"Maybe, maybe not," said Anna mysteriously.

A low wind whistled in the hedges and the sad cry of an owl echoed through the darkness as we walked slowly toward the farm. There was only the tiniest sliver of a moon, and the flashlight Mrs. Bell had lent Beth when she'd returned for the third head of garlic lit the way only about two feet ahead of us.

The blackness and silence of the night seemed ready to swallow us forever, and even Beth couldn't help feeling that somehow the night just didn't want us there. She knew Leo was scared because right from the beginning he'd clutched her hand and showed no signs of letting go. Teasdale seemed to be walking in some sort of trance, but at least he hadn't fainted—yet.

The main barn building was only a black silhouette against the empty-looking sky. Not even a star had come out that night to keep us company.

"This is the kind of night when dead people walk around," whispered Beth.

A cat darted suddenly across our path, and close by we thought we heard the sounds of branches being broken. A lone cow mooed mournfully from inside the barn, and from far off a dog barked for a moment.

We stationed ourselves by the main corral near the open area next to the barn and waited in silence. All three of us were fingering our garlic, and Teasdale appeared to have his head bowed in prayer.

It was one forty-five.

At one forty-seven a bird wailed.

At two o'clock a church bell from town sounded faintly from over the hills.

It was at two minutes past two that a dark form swept suddenly from the shadows to our left and dashed in silence across the open area toward the back of the barn. It moved so quickly that all we could get was a quick glimpse of what looked like a man, dressed in black, and wearing a long cape that swirled behind him as he ran.

We followed in pursuit and a moment later were approaching the back of the barn. We were just wondering where he had gone when the answer was provided for us: We heard once again, and from up close, that horrible scream. It echoed around the farm buildings, stopped as suddenly as it had started, and sounded oddly mechanical.

But there was nothing mechanical about the dark form

leaning over a black mass lying on the ground near one of the smaller corrals. We raced over, and when we were about fifteen feet away, Beth shined the flashlight toward the mysterious form.

The second the light fell on his face, Dracula immediately put his arm up to block the light from his eyes. His skin was amazingly pale and he had cruel-looking elongated eyebrows. The hands covering his eyes were clothed in white gloves, though the rest of his outfit, including the heavy cape with the high collar, was black, or maybe purple—it was difficult to tell by the limited light. But there could be no mistaking what he had smeared around his mouth and down his chin. It was blood.

When the light struck his face, Dracula gave an angry howl, licked his bloody lips, and showed his teeth—and they were large enough to frighten a shark! He then sneered in our direction and turned and quickly vanished into the night.

A moment later we were leaning over the dark form we'd seen on the ground. It was hardly a surprise to discover the body of a cow, stiff in death, with two teeth marks on its neck, around which was a small mass of dark blood, like a scab.

Teasdale, without even seeming to know what he was doing, reached out and patted the dead cow's head. "She's so cold," he murmured.

A bat darted over our heads, Leo started to cry, and Teasdale fainted. Beth closed her eyes and wished we hadn't started this investigation. Except for poor Rose's death, everything up to now had seemed almost like a game, what with interviewing people and sneaking around, looking for clues. Now it was different. We were in it over our heads—and with a real vampire for company.

For what else could it be?

Chapter Eight

A Busy Bunch

Everyone had a bad night. Needless to say, we three kids hardly slept a wink. Henhead reported her sinuses were hopelessly clogged after hearing the screams yet again and she wasn't alone in her distress. By the time we got down to breakfast, the dining room was abuzz with worried-looking but also excited people. Somehow they all seemed to know about our seeing Dracula. Over half of the people with whom we spoke told us they'd be leaving before lunch. As one woman said, "I'm not saying I believe all these rumors, but I'd rather not find out I'm wrong the hard way!" Another person told us, "I came here to regain my health—not lose my life!"

Of course Henhead couldn't make head or tail of what the people were talking about. It seemed she was the only person in Hidden Mountain Health Hotel who hadn't heard about Dracula being sighted the previous night.

So we had to tell her. Except we somehow neglected to tell her that we were the ones who had sighted him.

"My God!" exclaimed Henhead. "And here am I—with type A negative blood, surely among the world's rarest types! That vampire is probably making plans to bite my neck this very moment!"

We assured Henhead that Dracula seemed to prefer cows but she insisted on driving into town that very morning and buying some bug repellent. Henhead thought it would be effective in warding off vampires.

Poor Henhead was in such a rush to get to town that when she left the table she forgot to look where she was going, tripped over a waiter's leg, went flying through the air, and ended up lying on the floor like some forgotten doll. It would have been funny—especially since the waiter she bumped into had dropped a tray full of hot oatmeal—except that in falling she had somehow gashed her elbow which as a result was bleeding a bit.

Henhead saw the blood, probably thought the vampire was after her, and promptly fainted. By the time the hotel doctor had been found she had regained consciousness, though not her composure.

"Cover it up!" she was howling. "Cover it up!"

"Cover what up?" asked the doctor in that special voice doctors use when they're speaking with patients.

"My wound!" shrieked Henrietta. "Dracula might smell my blood and come for me! Cover it up!"

"Now, now, my dear," consoled the doctor, "even if there were such things as vampires, remember they only come out at night. And secondly, while it appears to be only a minor cut, it's still bleeding a bit—though not enough to warrant concern, mind you. We'll just have to wait until the wound stops bleeding and the blood around it coagulates—around five minutes or so if we apply a bit of pressure. Then I'll put some disinfectant on it and a nice clean bandage. How does that sound, dear?"

But Henhead didn't reply. She had fainted again.

It was exciting to be the center of attention. Everywhere we went, we heard people saying, "There they are! Those are the three kids who actually saw Dracula!" Some of the more forward guests came up and asked us about it. It was by this time useless to deny it, so Beth and Leo took turns answering because Teasdale doesn't like to talk to strangers very much. At first we enjoyed all the attention, but after around an hour of being celebrities we got tired of it. We tried hiding in one of the gloomier lounges, right behind a

58

glass case with a moth-eaten flying squirrel inside it, but an energetic woman with a cane found us, and we were scared she'd start hitting us with it if we didn't tell her all we knew.

The smallest lounge and the shadiest balcony proved no better; people seemed to find us wherever we went. So at last we decided to seek refuge with Mrs. Bell in her private chambers.

Mrs. Bell was slow to answer her door. We imagined she needed time to pull herself together. She certainly was brave. She managed to open the door with a smile and even look relatively happy, but we knew it was a front and it didn't take long for her to break down.

"I don't know how it all came out," she sighed. "But it seems everyone at Hidden Mountain knows about this Dracula episode, and they're checking out by the dozen! You know, children, mob psychology is an odd thing—once a crowd gets hold of an idea, it can spread like wildfire, no matter how unlikely the idea. I just wonder what the Board of Directors will think!"

"I know you said the board can decide things," commented Beth, "but can't you tell them what to do once in a while?"

"I wish I could, dear, but you see my husband, who loved this hotel and the land around it more than anything on earth, said in his will that certain decisions were in the hands of the Board of Directors and no one else."

"But why did he do that?" Leo wanted to know.

"Well," replied Mrs. Bell, "my husband had no way of knowing how long I'd wish or be able to run the hotel, so he wanted to be quite sure that if I were followed by an unscrupulous manager, he or she would have no way of doing things my husband wouldn't have liked."

"Such as?" wondered Beth.

"Such as stopping our policy of serving only fresh farm food and dairy products, or selling part of our land for developments. Things like that."

"That makes sense," Beth commented.

"Yes," said Mrs. Bell, "my husband thought of just about everything."

"Yeah," put in Leo, "everything except something like a vampire!"

"Don't remind me!" Mrs. Bell groaned. "You children have just about convinced me, but the Board of Directors is never going to believe this Dracula business. After all, it *is* rather hard to believe—and I doubt they'd wish to spend the night at the farm lying in wait as you dear children so bravely did. Even if they think the hotel can be saved, they're sure to think I'm incompetent to run it when they find out about the loss of the cows and the hotel's lack of profits."

"But Mrs. Bell," said Beth, "how can they blame you for lack of profits when there's a vampire hanging around your hotel? That's not your fault!"

"You know that and I know that, but they don't. How can I possibly prove there's a vampire? Teeth marks alone wouldn't do it. They might say I faked them somehow."

"Why don't you call in the police?" asked Leo. "They could investigate the whole thing!"

"I thought of that," Mrs. Bell explained. "But bringing in the police is just going to attract publicity for these awful vampire rumors—and that's the last thing I need now. I only hope I can make the board believe me, and give me another chance. But I'm scared it's too late— the meeting is scheduled for tomorrow afternoon. Oh, what will I do?"

At this point poor Mrs. Bell broke down and started sobbing loudly. As we watched in embarrassment, she put her face down in her arms and just shook with sorrow. Beth thought quickly and said:

"Don't cry, Mrs. Bell! Your problems are over!"

"They are?" said Leo.

"They are?" said Teasdale.

"They are?" said Mrs. Bell.

"They are," said Beth. "I've got a plan to beat all plans. If it's proof that dumb old board wants, it's proof that dumb old board'll get!"

"Please explain before I go insane," Teasdale pleaded.

"It's like this," Beth told her three rapt listeners. "Teasdale and Leo and I will return to the farm tonight—but not empty-handed! We'll bring a camera, and when Dracula shows his ugly face we'll photograph him! That'll be your proof! That board'll have to see your side of the story! They won't say it's your fault!"

"I declare I feel better already!" smiled Mrs. Bell. "And I just happen to have a Polaroid camera—and with a flash-cube in fine working order! Beth, you and your brothers may save me yet!"

Mrs. Bell's improved frame of mind did not extend to our aunt. Back in our rooms we found Henhead in great distress. She was pacing at a brisk clip and blowing her nose furiously. A trail of crumpled-up Kleenex made her progression around our suite easy to follow.

"Hen— I mean Aunt Henrietta," said Beth. "What's wrong?"

"What's wrong?" she gasped in reply. "What isn't wrong? I've had the world's worst day! My sinuses are seriously clogged and my migraine is worse than in years and I even stubbed a toe! And all because of that friend of yours you hate so much!"

"What?" we three kids said as one.

"That man Jon," Henrietta explained, "it's all his fault!"

"Would you mind telling us how?" asked Beth.

"Not at all," replied Henrietta. "It all started after I'd

61

bought the insect repellent and was heading home. At any rate, I thought I saw the same person I saw knock over the old lady the other day—you remember, the one I told you about. Well, I wanted to see whether or not he was that man Jon who came over to our table in the dining room. So I was looking so hard at him I neglected to look where I was driving—though only for a fraction of a second, mind you—and the next thing I knew all I could hear were screams and shouts and horns blowing. Really, the most dreadful racket. Of course I looked away from Jon—if it was Jon, and I think it was—and to my horror saw why all those rude people were shrieking and making so much noise. Was it my fault I was driving across the Town Common and heading for the Revolutionary War Memorial Statue?"

"So what happened?" gasped Beth. "Did you hit it?"

"Hit what?" Henhead asked.

"The statue!" replied Beth in exasperation.

"No, I did not," Henhead said primly. "What do you take me for? Just because I suffer ill health doesn't mean I can't drive a car! No, I managed to swerve and thus save an historic landmark from destruction. I can't imagine why Jon was so unpleasant about it."

"You mean about you not hitting the statue?" wondered Leo.

"No, about being run over," Henhead explained, just as though she ran over people a few times a week.

"You ran over Jon?" cried Beth.

"Not exactly 'ran over'; it was more like a sideswipe. It surely isn't my fault that Panhards are made with extra-strength thick steel and he was sent flying onto a park bench."

"Was he hurt?"

"Apparently he bruised one of his legs when he hit the bench. He did seem to have trouble walking afterward. And he was most unpleasant. He acted as though he didn't know

62

who I was. Quite rude—when all I wanted to do was apologize and see if I could be of assistance. After all, who knows more about how it feels to be ill or injured than myself?"

"Are you sure it was Jon?" asked Beth. "Did he have shiny brown hair?"

"Yes," stated Henrietta flatly. "His hair was shiny brown. Or was that his shoes? Perhaps it was his eyes . . . or did I hear someone mention he had attended Brown University, you know, that school in Providence, Rhode Island. Well, no matter: I am quite sure it was he. Now enough of this interrogation—I have to lie down. Go down to lunch without me. Eating after all this excitement would surely make me ill."

We didn't get down to the dining room until lunch was nearly over so we didn't have any choice as to where to sit. Since there were hardly any guests left, the kitchen staff had set only a limited number of tables. The others weren't even covered with tablecloths. It was quite depressing.

But what was even more depressing was that we had to sit with Mr. O'Hanrahan. He didn't look very happy about it either. His manners are worse than ours, even though our dad says we have the worst in the world.

It was the first time Teasdale had had a prolonged meeting with Mr. O'Hanrahan, and Beth could tell at a glance Teasdale wasn't taken with him. Teasdale has a certain trapped expression he puts on when he has to spend time with someone he dislikes.

We introduced Teasdale to Mr. O'Hanrahan and explained that Teasdale was also a writer, after which Mr. O'Hanrahan wanted to know if Teasdale wrote plays. Since Teasdale seemed to be refusing to speak, we told Mr. O'Hanrahan that Teasdale wrote poetry.

"Poetry!" sighed Mr. O'Hanrahan. "I never read it! I

never read plays either, as a matter of fact. You see, I'm much too busy writing them. You'll doubtless be interested to know that I have nearly completed the play which you begged me to read to you when you first visited my room. What a pity I don't have a copy on me."

"I think we'll get over it," said Beth. Then, to make conversation and also to get him off the topic of his play, Beth added, "I don't suppose you've been hearing those screams?"

"Yes, I have," Mr. O'Hanrahan told us. "I find them quite dull and most annoying. Dull because the mystery I'm writing is far more fascinating, and annoying because just last night I awoke with a brilliant idea of how to end Act Thirteen when that infernal howling drove it right out of my mind—a true loss to the world of theater!"

"I think they'll get over it," said Beth.

Finally lunch was over and we took our leave. As he said good-bye to Teasdale, Mr. O'Hanrahan bent over and said:

"Keep on writing, lad, and in time you just might write as well as I do!"

Teasdale looked away, a small flash of anger igniting his eyes, and mumbled:

"I stopped by the hotel library and read your last play;
If *I* wrote something that bad I'd throw it away!"

It isn't like Teasdale to be impolite, but even though Beth and Leo laughed themselves silly over Teasdale's little rhyme, I don't think Mr. O'Hanrahan even heard it. He's the kind of person who hears only what he wants to hear.

We'd been such a busy bunch all day we decided to take a nap before dinner so we'd be rested for the long night ahead. It was during her nap that Beth was sure she heard someone crying. She roused herself from sleep and sure

64

enough she was right. It was Teasdale. Beth got up as quickly as she could to join him, though by the time she got to him Leo was already there.

It turned out that discovering Dracula was even more upsetting for Teasdale than for us. Of course we all were upset—but Teasdale was *very* upset. He told us that when bad things like this happened, it made him miss our mom more than ever—which of course made Leo and me sad too. Teasdale also said that lots of times he felt sad just thinking about how much badness and unhappiness there was in the world; how mean people were to one another—with all the poverty and murders and crime, and old people having no one to care for them and little children going hungry. He said it made him feel even worse that on top of all this unhappiness that there'd exist something as evil as Dracula. Somehow it made him feel as though nothing would ever come out right. And even though Beth and Leo didn't feel exactly the same, we understood how Teasdale felt so we put our arms around him and told him we loved him. Because we do.

Chapter Nine

Fact or Fiction

There were three stars in the sky as we made our way to the farm that night. Teasdale said there was one for each of us, and that they were sent to protect us. Leo said he'd rather have a policeman. Beth said nothing at first; she was too busy thinking.

"Just think," said Beth, trying to make herself feel braver, "if I get a real photograph of Dracula, I'll be famous! Christopher Columbus! I bet we'll all be on the seven o'clock news—maybe even in the Guinness Book of World Records!"

"Yeah!" agreed Leo. "I'd say a vampire is second best only to a Martian!"

"I guess so," considered Beth. "I just wish I didn't feel so scared. How are you feeling, Teasdale?"

Teasdale reflected an instant, then said:

"Of course I'm frightened by something so dire—
It isn't so pleasant to meet a vampire!
But since going to meet him I seem to be,
Perhaps I can teach him to like poetry!"

"Hmmm," Beth responded, "I wouldn't put it past you! Still," she added, "I can't help but envying Henhead just a little bit—back in her room, sound asleep!"

"Forget it!" countered Leo. "Sound asleep with her head propped up on three pillows so her sinuses can drain, all those wads of cotton stuffed in her ears, that weird thing around her neck—I'd rather be out here!"

66

"You're right," agreed Beth.

As we approached the main barn a slight wind sprang up from the direction of the lake and blew away the clouds that had been covering the moon, so we had a bit more light. The wind also seemed to awaken the birds, and their cries sounded unbearably sad.

The night air was cool and as we settled down to keep watch by the main corral, we all shivered a bit. Teasdale had worn six sweaters so he was warm, but he was the only one. Beth was wishing she had worn gloves so her hands would stay warm, because she was responsible for taking the picture. She was just about to ask Teasdale if she could borrow the elbow-length dress gloves our uncle had sent him from Paris when suddenly a branch creaked, a twig broke, and footsteps neared the corral. A partridge took flight with its whirring cry of warning as the church bells once again tolled two o'clock.

It was time.

At the precise moment the bells ceased a shadow emerged from the shadows, and amid a swirling of capes we saw Dracula pass within six feet of us, walking slowly and with a slight limp. Beth had planned to wait to photograph him until he stood still, at least for a moment, but Leo and Teasdale ruined that plan. It hardly needs saying that when Dracula suddenly passed so near to us Teasdale fainted— but at least he did it quietly. Leo was so taken aback that without warning he let out a horrified little shriek—something he's been embarrassed about ever since. The shriek startled Dracula, who looked angrily in our direction, gave a horrible laugh, and to our panic started to come toward us!

Luckily Leo had the presence of mind to start waving his garlic around and Beth had the presence of mind to snap a quick photo—she hardly had time to aim the camera. I can't say anything about Teasdale's presence of mind because he was still in a faint.

We weren't sure whether it was the garlic or the suddenness of the flashcube which sent Dracula stumbling off into the darkness, but at least he did, and was gone as quickly as he had come.

Beth and Leo breathed a sigh of relief, Teasdale revived without even a drop of water being dumped on his head (Beth had brought a special canteen just for that purpose), and we all huddled together around the small camera, waiting breathlessly for the picture to come out. The longest sixty seconds of our lives passed and finally the camera seemed to click and spring to life and the blank picture came sliding out. Beth detached it and while Leo shined the light on it we all watched it develop.

Slowly the picture appeared. When it was fully developed we examined it closely. Even by the dim gleam of the flashlight there could be little doubt as to what the picture proved.

What had nagged so long at the back of Beth's mind sprang to the front. And she knew there was no such thing as Dracula—he was a fraud, just someone in disguise.

And this photo showed who.

"I'm afraid this photograph only proves what I had feared all along," sighed Mrs. Bell. "I just hope we're not too late to save the hotel—the loss of revenue thanks to this prank has hurt us badly. I fear the board might wish to— well, better not to think about it. We'll have to hope for the best!"

It was mid-morning, and after sleeping late we had made our way to Mrs. Bell's office. We had entered in great excitement, crying, "We've got it! We've got it!"

"Got what?" Mrs. Bell had asked.

"The photograph of Dracula," Beth had replied. "And prepare yourself for a shock!"

Mrs. Bell had reached for the photo and had examined it in silence, the three of us gathered around her, gazing with pride at the good job we had done.

It wasn't the world's clearest photograph, but it was clear enough. It showed a man full-face. It seemed likely from the photo that the extreme pallor of his face was due to talcum powder, and the length of his eyebrows to makeup. And the red around his mouth didn't really look like blood—and anyway, Dracula was on his way to the barn and hadn't even killed a cow yet, so how could he be all bloody? He was wearing a hooded garment and I guess when he turned around so suddenly after Leo screamed the hood had fallen from his head revealing his face. And the face in the picture was Jon's.

"Yes," Mrs. Bell continued, sounding pleased, "I believe I told you I kept Jon on only because my late husband was so fond of him. I never trusted the man and can only imagine he did this dreadful deed to drive me out of business—I know he was furious with me for having given him his notice! But imagine taking this kind of revenge! The man must be insane!"

"That's for sure!" agreed Beth. "But at least he'll be spending the next few years in prison—my picture'll put him behind bars for sure!"

"Why don't you call the police to come and arrest Jon right away?" demanded Leo.

"Yes," said Teasdale, "do call the police now—before he hurts another cow!"

"Don't fret, you dear children; I know just how to act," replied Mrs. Bell. "You see, I am still hesitant to call in the police for the reason I mentioned the other day . . . although I do believe we now have all the evidence against Jon we need, thanks to you children—you've been more help than I can say. I'll present this information to the board this afternoon and let them decide our best course of action as concerns Jon. But don't worry: I'll have Bill or Frank keep an eye on Jon from now on so he won't get into any more mischief!"

"Ooh," said Beth. "It still gives me the creeps to think about Jon being on the loose till the board shows up!"

"Better Jon on the loose than a vampire!" smiled Mrs. Bell.

The news about Jon being the vampire had yet to find its way around the hotel. And the people we told weren't sure if we were telling the truth or making it up.

"You're probably just saying that because you're friendly with Mrs. Bell," one man told us, adding, "my wife and I never believed that vampire business anyway—but we're still checking out this afternoon. Vampire or no vampire, the atmosphere in this hotel has become most unpleasant. And we've told all our friends not to come here!"

It seemed that so many people had told their friends not to come to Hidden Mountain we were sure that poor Mrs. Bell didn't have a chance to save her hotel, even without a vampire.

"That mean old board'll close it for sure," Beth was saying when a loud raucous laugh from around the corner in the lounge where we'd been standing let us know our friend Mrs. Fillipelli was in the neighborhood.

"I'm glad she hasn't left yet," remarked Beth as the three of us raced to find her.

"Land sakes alive!" she exclaimed as we came charging around the corner. "If it isn't my old friends, the Three Musketeers!" And she gave Teasdale a friendly slap that knocked the wind out of him for a good fifteen minutes.

Mrs. Fillipelli was dressed in the largest pair of blue jeans Beth had ever set eyes on. She was also wearing a pair of large hiking boots, a lumber jacket that looked big enough for an elephant, and a little blue beret perched on her curly brown hair at a rakish angle.

"I'm going for a hike!" she confided. "I've never been on one before! I'm going to climb that hill right off the lake—and have I packed the world's most delicious lunch! I thought I deserved a treat after what happened last night— it was so upsetting!"

"You mean about Jon?" asked Beth.

"How'd you know about that, honey?" replied Mrs. Fillipelli. "I haven't told a soul!"

"We didn't have to be told," Beth said. "We were there!"

"Where?" asked Mrs. Fillipelli and Beth started to think that maybe all the extra weight she'd been carrying had affected her brain.

"With Jon, of course," explained Beth. "We were with Jon when he was pretending to be Dracula and we even took his picture!"

"I don't know what you're talking about," Mrs. Fillipelli answered. "It was Jon who insulted me last night when I was visiting the freezer for a snack—and you kids were nowhere in sight!"

"Of course not," said Leo. "We were at the farm!"

"Really!" exclaimed Mrs. Fillipelli. "This is more confusing than talking to Luigi's sister-in-law Julietta! Mama mia! Is she crazy!"

"It *is* kind of confusing," agreed Beth. "Why don't you just tell us exactly what you're talking about and then we'll tell you what we're talking about."

"Fine," said Mrs. Fillipelli. "It's like this: Dinner last night was so skimpy I woke up in the middle of the night and just *had* to have a bite or two of ice cream—preferably chocolate chip but I wasn't particular—so I went down to the freezer. Remember, I told you kids I knew how to get there and get it open? Well, who should I meet there but that good-for-nothing Jon I'd heard had been so mean to

71

little Teasdale! And, can you believe it, he had the nerve to tell me that the freezer was off-limits to guests and I should get out of the kitchen! Me, Sofia Maria Giana della Rosa Fillipelli, who's spent more than three-quarters of my life in a kitchen—being ordered out of one by a farmhand who probably doesn't even know the difference between vermicelli and linguine!"

"Sounds like Jon—he's a guy whose manners are gone," rhymed Teasdale.

"That's for sure," put in Leo. "Just one question: What time did you see Jon?"

"I know exactly," Mrs. Fillipelli told us, "because I looked at my watch when I entered the kitchen—I always like to know what time it is when I'm eating."

"So what time was it?" asked Beth.

"Two o'clock on the dot," Mrs. Fillipelli responded.

"Are you sure?" demanded a shaken Leo.

"Of course I'm sure—do you think I'd fool around with something as important as eating? It was two o'clock exactly—I'd stake my appetite on it! Now what was it you wanted to tell me about?"

"I'm not so sure anymore," Beth replied slowly. "I, um, think it can wait till after your hike."

"Fine, I'll be back in the afternoon . . . I'm so looking forward to my day outdoors—just me, nature, and a knapsack full of food!" chuckled Mrs. Fillipelli. "Though I must admit whatever it was you were saying about Jon sounded very intriguing! But you can tell me more later."

"Do you realize what this means?" gasped Leo as soon as Mrs. Fillipelli had waddled off. "It means it couldn't have been Jon we saw! Maybe it was a real vampire that just happened to look like Jon! After all, Jon does have a kind of mean face and so would a vampire—at least I think one would!"

"Maybe Mrs. Fillipelli was wrong," suggested Beth.

"About food? C'mon!" countered Leo. "If Mrs. Fillipelli says she was eating a snack at two o'clock and saw Jon, then she did. We'd better warn Mrs. Bell that there really is a vampire on the loose! She might not have someone guarding the cows and let them wander in the corrals and who knows how many Dracula might kill if he had the chance!"

"I think we should ask a few more questions, first," Beth responded.

"What sort of questions?" Leo wanted to know.

"Let's try to find out if Jon also has an alibi for the night before last. If by chance someone has seen him both nights, then we know it wasn't Jon at the farm last night. It would have to be someone else, unless there really is a vam—, a— Boy, all of a sudden I hate to say the word!"

"We might as well try it," agreed Leo. "After all, Dracula won't go after any of the cows till dark and it's only mid-morning. We've got tons of time. Sound OK to you, Teasdale?"

"First the vampire is Jon and then he is real—it makes me feel worse than I ever did feel," responded our poet brother, as he turned very pale but managed not to faint.

Since it was lunchtime, we decided to go to the dining room and see what we could learn there from the remaining guests. It was Beth who came up with the idea of asking people everything they'd done and everyone they'd spoken with for the last three days. And though there weren't that many people left, it took at least an hour to do all the interviewing, even though we split up.

But luck was with us. When we regrouped we had found out a lot—but boy was it confusing!

Mr. O'Hanrahan said that the night when the shrieks of the cow being killed had made him lose his brilliant ending to Act Thirteen, he had gone to the main lobby to see if he could get a drink, or at least find someone to talk to. To his annoyance, the bar was shut and the lobby vacant. But he did catch a glimpse of someone walking at the far end of the lobby who looked like Jon—though he wasn't totally sure.

"Hmmm," said Leo. "This gives Jon an alibi for both nights! I bet there really is a vampire!"

"Yeah," answered Beth, "except for one thing: Mr. O'Hanrahan is about the most unobservant person in the universe! And I found out something else that proves it still might be Jon. I chatted with Henhead—who by the way said she'd caught the most dreadful cold—and she reminded me of something we'd forgotten. Something so obvious you'll die when you hear it!"

"So tell me!"

"OK: Think back for a sec to last night, when we saw what we thought was Dracula, and then try to remember something special about the way he was moving. Remember—he *limped!*"

"So?"

"So remember what Henhead told us, all about her hitting Jon with the Panhard, and him having hurt one leg, and having trouble walking afterward? That's why Dracula limped last night! It was Jon, and his leg still hurt!"

"Sounds reasonable—except for one thing," said Leo slowly.

"Namely?"

"I spoke to Anna—and she swore that at just around the same time Henhead said she was running over Jon, he was taking her on a tour of the farm—she'd been wondering how much farming had changed since her childhood on a farm in Russia."

"That doesn't sound like Jon," said Beth. "And anyway, you said Anna said 'around the same time': That doesn't

74

mean *exactly* the same time. And besides, Anna's pretty old—maybe she got mixed up."

"I don't think Anna's the kind to get mixed up," countered Leo. "But it is true that Anna did say 'around'—I mean, just fifteen minutes or so would give Jon time to get back here from town. When you come right down to it, Henhead's much more likely to get mixed up, you know: Remember she didn't know if she'd hit a guy with brown hair, brown eyes, or brown shoes! And about Jon—Anna said she thinks Jon is actually a really nice guy—just a bit grumpy on the outside."

"Well who knows!" groaned Beth. "Every time we get one piece of information, another piece comes along and contradicts it! But I still say it's Jon—Mrs. Fillipelli just made a mistake about the time. Maybe she sat on her watch! Though it sure seems as though Jon is good at being in two places at one time, doesn't it?"

"Doesn't what?" asked an old voice. Beth looked up to see Pops Simon, an unlit cigar in his mouth and a candy cane stuck behind his left ear.

"I said it was impossible for one person to be in two places at one time," said Beth.

"Not if there're two of them," replied Pops. "People do come in twos, threes, even sixes I hear—though they're still one of a kind, no matter how many show up!"

"He's the one who's one of a kind," remarked Beth after Pops had walked off to find a pine tree to hang his candy cane on. "He's as crazy as that sister-in-law Mrs. Fillipelli mentioned."

"*I* think so—but that reminds me of something else Anna said," Leo replied. "She said he's not half as crazy as he wants people to think he is."

"Well, I think the whole world is crazy, at least around here!" said Beth. "Vampires who are vampires, vampires

75

who aren't vampires, people in two places at one time, crazy people who aren't crazy—what are we going to do?"

"I think we'd better go talk to Mrs. Bell—she might have an idea," said Leo. "At the very least it's real important for her to know all this new stuff about Jon we've discovered—and before the board meeting. And she also better know there just might be a real vampire!"

Pops Simon

Chapter Ten

Bertil's Book

"This changes everything," sighed Mrs. Bell. "It seems you're telling me one thing—all about Jon's alibis—but the photo you took is telling me something else!"

Poor Mrs. Bell—she was taking this new development hard. Beth had never seen her more upset and nervous.

"Don't worry, Mrs. Bell," Beth consoled her. "We're all confused too. I think Leo still thinks there really is a vampire and I still think it's Jon. I'm not sure what Teasdale thinks."

"I don't care if Dracula's Jon or a runaway gnome," reported Teasdale, "I just wish I were safely at home."

"I'm sure you do, dear," said Mrs. Bell as she scratched the back of her neck, lost in thought. "This really does change everything," she murmured half to herself and then added, "Now let me get this straight. Your aunt thinks she bumped into Jon in town and had seen him there before. Well, she might be confused—she does tend that way. Now, what were the other new pieces of information?"

"One was what Mr. O'Hanrahan told us," answered Beth. "Remember he said he'd seen Jon two nights ago—when we thought we saw him disguised as Dracula."

"I think we can discount that," Mrs. Bell pronounced. "Mr. O'Hanrahan was probably just incorrect—that man is really quite unobservant."

"Then there was what Anna said . . ." began Leo.

"But didn't you say Anna wasn't exactly sure about the time?" replied Mrs. Bell. "I don't think we need concern ourselves with her . . ."

77

"And what about the limp?" demanded Beth. "Doesn't that prove it's Jon?"

"It's certainly strong evidence—but it's not proof enough to say it was Jon. After all, your aunt wasn't even positive it was Jon she hit."

"Doesn't Mrs. Fillipelli's information throw any light on the situation?" rhymed Teasdale.

"Actually, Mrs. Fillipelli's evidence is the only thing that really points toward Jon's possible innocence. Of course, she might have been mistaken. Anyone can misread a watch—especially late at night, when they're tired. But if Mrs. Fillipelli was right, and it wasn't Jon at the farm, as much as I dislike the man, I still wouldn't want to see him slandered! Um, do you think Mrs. Fillipelli will speak to anyone about what she saw?"

"Not a chance," said Beth. "She's spending the day alone hiking so she won't be speaking with anybody."

"And when might she be returning from her hike?" Mrs. Bell wanted to know.

"Not till the afternoon," answered Leo.

"So she won't get back before I, uh, have to leave for the board meeting . . ." Mrs. Bell said. "Are you quite sure about this?"

"Of course," Beth replied.

"Fine," said Mrs. Bell. "But if Mrs. Fillipelli was right—Heaven help us, but we have to consider the possibility we really do have a vampire on our hands! After all, while your photo certainly looks like Jon, we can't be entirely sure. Maybe Dracula happens to resemble Jon—stranger things have happened I'm sure!"

"That's what I think!" stated Leo. "There *is* a vampire!"

"And I say it's Jon!" countered Beth. "And *I'm* right!"

"Now, now—let's not argue! I have to think . . . there must be a way to resolve this. Ah! I've got it!"

Mrs. Bell stood up and quickly walked over to a large

78

wooden bookshelf at the far end of the room. She stood in front of it, looking from shelf to shelf until she found what she was looking for.

When she returned to her chair she was holding a large, very old leather-bound book with gilt pages and a fancy title embossed on the front in gold letters. It read *Vampir-Legende*.

"What's the book?" wondered Beth.

"It's an old German book Bill found many years ago. It was written by a man named Bertil von Göttenburg who at one time was one of the world's foremost experts on what was called unexplained phenomena—things such as ghosts, extrasensory perception—and vampires. Anyway, Bill located this book—the title in German means 'Vampire Legends'—and it's an overview of many of Europe's vampire legends."

"So how does this help us?" demanded Leo. "We're not in Europe!"

"Of course not, dear. However, this book does have a small section on other parts of the world, and it mentions Hidden Mountain! Or, to be more precise, Mount Sang. Now, where is that page?"

Mrs. Bell began leafing through the book and when she got to the right page and opened the book wide to read, a piece of paper came fluttering out and landed at Beth's feet.

"It's a note from Bill," remarked Beth as Mrs. Bell took the note from her hand before she could read more.

"Of course," said Mrs. Bell, "Bill lent me this book shortly after he found it. Like Bill, I speak a touch of German and wanted to know just what we might be up against. Here it is: 'A most unusual vampire legend has been collected in the hills of New Hampshire where French explorers even named a local mountain Mount Sang (or "blood") as a result of all the vampire sightings emanating from this locale. A pile of rocks on the top of this mountain is known as Crow Peak be—'"

"Bill already told us all this," interrupted Leo. "Why don't you skip a bit?"

"Fine," said Mrs. Bell. "Um, here we go: 'While there have been no reported sightings of a vampire in recent years, a legend persists that should the vampire walk again he will announce his intentions by placing a candle at the window of the small stone hut on Pine Peak, just to the west of Mount Sang. It is this abandoned hut which local residents claim was the vampire's hiding place during daylight hours, although no proof to support this claim has ever come to light. The disused hut is located just beyond Dead Man's Drop.' That's all it says."

"Do—do you believe all this?" asked Leo.

"I don't," Beth stated flatly. "I still say it's Jon. Whoever heard of a real vampire?"

"Don't be dumb!" responded Leo. "If there can be UFOs and Martians, why can't there be vampires?"

Mrs. Bell started talking again before Beth could come up with an answer to Leo's question. "I know you children have done so much for me already, I hate to ask you for anything else."

"Ask away," said Beth.

"I know it's a lot to ask, but do you think the three of you could visit the abandoned house that von Göttenburg mentions—just to be sure? I know I won't be able to rest till I know for sure there's no candle in the window! Except for Bill, I'm the only one who's seen the *Vampir Legende* book—so only a real vampire would know about the candle."

"You want us to pay a house call on Dracula!" Leo responded. "No way!"

"Oh, relax, Leo," said Beth. "It's broad daylight—nothing can happen to us. Vampires only come out after it's dark!"

"But it's already almost lunchtime!" moaned Leo. "How long a hike is it to this dump, anyway?"

"It used to take all day, dear," said Mrs. Bell sweetly, "but now, since we put that bridge up over Dead Man's Drop, it's only a hike of an hour or so. You will do it, won't you? I just don't know how I could attend this afternoon's board meeting and argue for the life of the hotel without knowing for sure if there really was a vampire!"

The only disagreement came from Teasdale. When he heard that Dead Man's Drop was a ravine forty feet deep and he'd have to cross it by means of a small narrow wooden bridge without railings, Teasdale refused to even think about going. He is horribly afraid of heights.

"I know just how you feel," sympathized Mrs. Bell. "I too suffer from acrophobia. But if when you're crossing the bridge you walk in the middle, with Beth holding one hand and Leo the other, I'm sure you'll be just fine."

This advice calmed Teasdale's fears. After we'd all agreed to go, Mrs. Bell made us promise not to tell anyone where we were going or why. She said if it turned out there was no Dracula this information about her asking us to do this might prove very embarrassing—especially if the board should hear of it.

We promised, and Mrs. Bell said it was vital to leave immediately—we didn't have a moment to waste if we wanted to get back with our findings before the board meeting started at four o'clock. And in case the hike took a bit longer, we certainly didn't want to be there after dark, now did we?

That question hardly needed answering, so Mrs. Bell said she'd just dash upstairs and get a good map of our route and be back in a minute.

Leo and Beth spent the next five or six minutes of Mrs. Bell's absence trying to decide if we believed what this von Göttenburg had said. Beth didn't, Leo did, and since

81

Teasdale had gone to the bathroom we couldn't find out what his opinion was.

"Sorry to be so long," said Mrs. Bell, "but I just couldn't lay my hands on the map—it turned out to be just where I was sure it wasn't. Now—let me see . . ."

The hike, at least as far as we could tell from the map, wouldn't be too difficult. We didn't even think it would tire Teasdale. We had to walk behind the hotel, to the right of the lake, through the small foothills and, bearing right, up to Pine Peak. Mrs. Bell promised us the path was well-marked. About two-thirds of the way up Pine Peak was a deep gulley or ravine, Dead Man's Drop, over which was the wooden bridge that had so frightened Teasdale. And just beyond the bridge was the stone house.

"What's up?" came a voice, and we wheeled around to see Bill, who seemed to have come from nowhere. Mrs. Bell told Bill what we were doing and he said we were great kids. He then said he had to get back to the farm and ran off.

"Remember," Mrs. Bell called after us as we were leaving, "this is our secret—yours, mine, and Bill's. Don't tell a soul! Promise?"

"Promise!" we called back and headed down the long corridor and off to adventure.

"This just might be fun," commented Beth.

"Yeah," agreed Leo. "No one can stop us now!"

But we hadn't counted on Teasdale!

We hadn't even made it to the back door when Teasdale suddenly stopped dead in his tracks and refused to budge.

"No—I won't go!" he told us.

"Then we'll go without you," Leo answered crossly.

"If you go without me, I'll tell ev'ryone I see!"

This was when Beth stepped in. She's very experienced at dealing with Teasdale and had figured out that he must have something quite important on his mind to act in this fashion.

"OK, Teas," she said. "Tell us what's going on."

Teasdale took a deep breath, looked around nervously, and then explained: "When I went off to the bathroom alone . . . I saw Mrs. Bell on the telephone!"

"So?" said Leo. "It's not against the law to make a phone call, is it?"

"I don't get it either, Teas," added Beth. "Could you please explain a bit more—and not in rhyme, if you don't mind."

"What I'm trying to say is that when Mrs. Bell was making the phone call, she already had the map in her hand!"

"So what?" said Leo. "Who cares?"

"Wait a minute!" exclaimed Beth. "I see what Teasdale's getting at. Mrs. Bell said she was gone so long 'cause it took her a long time to find the map—but that wasn't true. Christopher Columbus! She was lying to us!"

"Oh, come on!" disagreed Leo. "I think you're both jumping the gun! Everyone knows how worried Mrs. Bell has been lately—I bet she just forgot all about the phone call. Or maybe it was a personal phone call about something she didn't want to tell us about."

"Maybe," Beth replied, "but if she was lying about taking so long to find the map, then she could be lying about everything else, too!"

"But why would she do that?" demanded Leo. "She's our friend!"

"That's the part I can't figure out, but then you can't always tell who your friends are. At least that's what our dad says," commented Beth. "And the more I think about it, the more it seems pretty weird that that book just happened to be in German—which none of us can read."

"But I still want to know why she'd lie," repeated Leo.

"Beats me," Beth told him. "Maybe Mrs. Bell is in league

with Jon or something—maybe she and Jon just pretend to hate each other! Maybe that book has nothing to do with Mount Sang and Crow Peak and all! I'm with Teasdale— I'm not trusting Mrs. Bell anymore until I know exactly what was written in that book! If it really is about Crow Peak and all, then I'll believe everything else Mrs. Bell was saying."

"But what about the phone call?" countered Teasdale.

"If everything else is true, then I agree with Leo that it's probably not important," replied Beth.

"But how can we tell?" wondered Leo.

"There's no need to stand around squirmin'," announced Teasdale. "Let's just find someone who knows how to read German!"

We put our heads together and thought. We remembered that Anna could speak Russian, Mrs. Fillipelli could speak Italian, and Teasdale could speak French—but no one could speak German.

Leo remembered Mrs. Bell saying that Bill could speak German, but Beth said if there was a chance Mrs. Bell wasn't on the level, then Bill might not be either. Maybe they were in this together—although why we couldn't even begin to imagine.

But one thing we didn't even need to try to imagine was how awful we suddenly felt. It seemed as though there wasn't a single grown-up we could trust. Not only didn't we like facing a possible vampire on our own, we didn't like not knowing if our friends Mrs. Bell and Bill were truly our friends.

"Too bad our dad isn't here," Leo said. "We could sure use a lawyer at a time like this!"

"You know," considered Beth after a moment's pause, "there *is* someone we all know who speaks German—the question is: Do we want to ask this person?"

"I'd say the question is: Do we have a choice?" responded

84

Leo. "Who is your mysterious German-speaking stranger we all know?"

"Henhead," replied Beth to stunned silence.

When we got to our suite we found Henhead taking a nap. We tried to rouse her, but she protested that she was positive she had a touch of the flu and wanted to sleep. Beth could tell from Leo's expression that he was thinking Henhead was the wrong person to ask. It had taken a lot of convincing on Beth and Teasdale's part to get Leo to agree not only to break our promise to Mrs. Bell not to tell anyone, but to break our promise for Henhead.

"Get up anyway!" said Beth. "We need your help! And in a hurry!"

"You do?" Henhead asked in a surprised but pleased-sounding voice as she got out of bed and found a seat on a chair. "So what is it?"

We told her the entire story.

"My God!" exclaimed Henhead when we had finished— and then started to cry.

"Hen— I mean Aunt Henrietta, don't cry!" said Beth, going over and giving her a little hug. "Nobody's been hurt! We're all right! And I bet there isn't any vampire, and Mrs. Bell wasn't really lying!"

"That—that's not why I'm crying," sobbed Henhead.

"Then why *are* you crying?" we wanted to find out.

"Because I'm happy" was the confusing answer.

"Happy?"

"It's hard to explain," Henhead went on. "But you see, ever since we've been here you kids have hardly spent a moment with me—you always seemed to have better things to do than be with me. I couldn't help but think you didn't like me! It really hurt my feelings! At least now I know you were on the scent of a simply fascinating mystery— how well I recall when your father and I were children we

85

got into such trouble because we were sure the downstairs neightbors were counterfeiters!"

"Were they?"

"No—in fact they were policemen, and they didn't take very kindly to being trailed by two giggling children!"

"You and our dad did that?" we gasped.

"And more!" smiled Aunt Henrietta. "But you know, what you're involved in now doesn't seem made-up. There is something going on—and we're going to get to the bottom of it or I'll eat my hat!"

We could hardly believe our ears, not to mention our eyes. We'd never seen Henhead so lively and excited.

"You think you feel well enough to help us?" wondered Beth.

"Well," sighed Henrietta, "my head *does* ache—but no matter. I can lie down later. We have to get going!"

Minutes later we were down the hall from Mrs. Bell's office. Aunt Henrietta had turned out to be pretty smart when it came to planning spy missions.

Here's what we did:

Aunt Henrietta and Leo stationed themselves just to the left of Mrs. Bell's office, in a recess in the wall so she couldn't see them. Teasdale stationed himself around the corner to the right, facedown on the floor as though he had fainted, and after all this stationing was done Beth came charging up to Mrs. Bell's door screaming, "Help! Help! Mrs. Bell!"

The office door flew open and Mrs. Bell appeared. When she heard Beth's news that Teasdale had fainted down the hall and Beth couldn't revive him, she and Beth trotted quickly down the hall to where Teasdale was lying in his supposed faint.

The second they turned the corner, Aunt Henrietta and Leo raced into the office and Leo opened the *Vampir Leg-*

ende book to the right page so our aunt could read it. She stood there in silence, concentrating on the German, and finally nodded. "Fine," she whispered. "Let's get out of here!"

Our aunt had told Teasdale to count up to three hundred before he revived but I think he must have gone up to three thousand. But it worked. He de-fainted and claimed to be feeling great, and Mrs. Bell went back to her office.

"You're still going to do me that favor, aren't you?" she asked.

"Sure, Mrs. Bell—Teasdale's just fine now. I'll scout up Leo and we'll be off!"

"You dear children," said Mrs. Bell, shutting the office door behind her.

"She wasn't lying," pronounced Aunt Henrietta when we had regrouped in our suite. "The book said exactly what Mrs. Bell said it did. At least we know she's on the level."

"Right," agreed Beth. "But that's about all we know."

"Yeah—I guess we're going to have to hike up to that house old Bertil was talking about," was Leo's opinion.

"Never!" snorted our aunt with fury. "It's much too dangerous! Who knows what might be lurking up in those hills! In Ireland I heard all about banshees and pookas—the people there really believe in them! So maybe there just might be something like a vampire. I mean, after all, all these legends must have started for a reason! No—I'd never forgive myself should something happen to you—never!"

"Relax, Aunt Henrietta, nothing's going to happen to us in broad daylight," Beth reassured her. "If there is a vampire, which I don't believe for a minute, he can't come out until sundown—and if there isn't, why then there's nothing to worry about anyway! Right?"

"I guess so," said Aunt Henrietta doubtfully. "But you'll

87

promise to be extra careful and come back promptly without dawdling?"

"Sure—and if we're going to come back at all we'd better leave. C'mon, boys!"

Aunt Henrietta made us take enough extra clothing, food, and medicine to stock a small army. She even insisted we carry a rope! We each had to carry a small pack to fit it all in, even Teasdale. We didn't like carrying all this weight, but it was the only way our aunt would agree to let us go.

As we bid our aunt good-bye at the door of the suite, Beth asked, "So what are you going to do this afternoon? Go on with your nap?"

"Well," said our aunt after some consideration, "you know, I would dearly love a nap, but no—there's something else I'm going to do!"

"Like what?" wondered Leo.

"Like it has something to do with all this vampire business," she replied. "It's a little something I remember that's the tiniest bit, well—odd, shall we say. And I just want to look into it, that's all."

"Won't you at least tell us what it is?" Beth asked.

"We'll compare notes when we all get back—it should be by late afternoon I'd say" was all our aunt would tell us. "Now let's all get going—and remember: Be careful! You never know what's going to happen!"

Truer words were never spoken.

Chapter Eleven

The House on the Hill

It was a lovely afternoon for a hike. The sun warmed our shoulders as we walked and a slight wind cooled our faces. Teasdale spotted a large number of birds and Beth was able to pick a decent-looking bouquet of wild flowers. Leo wondered if Beth were planning to give the flowers to Dracula, which wasn't exactly what Beth had in mind. The truth was that picking wild flowers reminded both Beth and Teasdale of our mom—gathering flowers and arranging them in small bouquets in delicate vases around our house was one of her special delights.

The map Mrs. Bell had given us was easy to follow and we didn't have to wonder if we were going the right way to get to Pine Peak. We did, of course, wonder what we would find once we crossed Dead Man's Drop and saw the abandoned stone house. What if there really was a candle in the window? The nearer we got to Dead Man's Drop the easier it seemed to believe we'd find a candle and know there really was a vampire! Perhaps it was the fact that all Beth's flowers wilted so soon, even for wild flowers, or maybe it was Teasdale mentioning that there weren't any more birds around this part of the mountain. Even Leo, who rarely seems to notice if he's hot, cold, or freezing, said this part of the hike made him feel chilly in his bones. In short we were getting the same creepy feeling of not being wanted by the place we were in we had gotten at the farm the first time we sighted Dracula. We also kept getting the uncomfortable sensation we were being followed.

When, according to the map, we were around half a mile

from Dead Man's Drop, we stopped for a snack. As we munched on the nuts and raisins our aunt had made us bring, we discussed the whole Dracula business for at least the two millionth time.

"So, Beth," began Leo, "do you still think it was Jon?"

Beth considered a moment before answering. "I'm not totally sure—the more I think about it, the more I believe there couldn't be a vampire. But then I think about Mrs. Fillipelli seeing Jon in the kitchen at the same time we saw Dracula—at least, maybe she did. So once in a while, for a second or two, I think there just might be a Dracula!"

"Yeah," agreed Leo, "and remember, in nearly every Dracula movie I've ever seen, Drac's sort of dark and mysterious-looking but kind of handsome, too. And that's how Jon looks. So that's why I think that in the photo we thought Drac was Jon in disguise—when actually it was really a real vampire! And there we were—only six feet away!"

"What about this idea: Maybe Jon is a vampire!" gasped Beth.

"That's a good—" Leo started to say but then stopped. "No," he said, "that's impossible. The one thing we know for sure about vampires is that they can't go out in the daylight. So while there might be a vampire for real—the way I think there is—or Dracula might be Jon in disguise—the way you think—one thing we can be sure about is that Jon isn't a real vampire."

"Makes sense," commented Beth. "What do you think, Teasdale?" But Teasdale just answered something about there being more things in heaven and earth than Horatio could dream about in his philosophies. This didn't mean much to Beth or Leo until later when we learned Teasdale had been quoting Shakespeare.

Our snack being over, we repacked our knapsacks and started to head out. Teasdale wanted to know why we couldn't just leave our packs where we'd snacked and return for them on the way back.

"My knapsack's as heavy as lead," he explained, "if I carry it longer I know I'll be dead!"

But we told Teasdale to dry up and keep on walking, knapsack and all—and it was a good thing we did.

"You know," announced Beth, "at least I no longer feel as though we're being followed!"

"That's good!" cheered Leo.

"Not really—*now* I keep hearing somebody ahead of us!"

Dead Man's Drop was about half an hour farther up Pine Peak, and the higher we climbed the more spectacular the view became. We could see mountain after mountain on the horizon, and below us, through the pine trees that lined our route, we caught a glimpse of the lake as it sparkled in the afternoon sun. And just beyond it we saw, tiny in the distance, Hidden Mountain Health Hotel. It looked so peaceful from far away we could hardly believe the excitement it had gone through in the last few days.

"You know," observed Beth, "I'm really starting to see why our mom liked this place so much!"

"We're almost there!" cried Leo, and Beth turned from the view and her thoughts and looked ahead, through more pines, until she too could see a bridge across a large ravine and beyond it, also obscured by pines, a small broken-down stone house.

We all dashed forward to see if we could catch sight of a candle, but the house was too far away for us to get a good view. What we could see was how deep a ravine it was that the small wooden bridge crossed, and why it was named Dead Man's Drop. As Beth peered down its banks to the rock-covered bottom a good forty feet down, she wondered if anyone had ever fallen into it, or if the name had just been chosen after imagining what would happen if someone did.

The bridge was wooden, made of planks laid horizontally across two thick wooden crossbeams that spanned the ravine and were secured in the earth on either end. It looked old but appeared strong.

"OK, boys, let's go!" said Beth. "And let's hurry—I keep feeling again as though someone's following us!"

"Make up your mind!" exclaimed Leo. Then, after he'd taken a good look at the bridge, he added, "Wow! This'll be just like walking in space!"

"Let's hope all's well on the other side!" responded Beth, squinting her eyes to get a better view of the abandoned house on the far side of the ravine. "C'mon, Teasdale!" she shouted. "We're waiting! Hurry up or you'll have to cross by yourself!"

"I'll be there in a second, sweet sister of mine!" called Teasdale from a pine grove a few paces back, "I just thought I saw a rare bird in this big old—" But Teasdale never finished the sentence—instead we heard the sounds of boughs bending and scraping, followed by a horrified series of shrieks from Teasdale, and then silence.

"They got him!" shouted Beth, and she and Leo raced to the pine grove where Teasdale's shrieks had sounded. *Please—may he be all right,* Beth prayed to herself as she sprinted toward the trees. *I know Leo says he can't come out in the daylight, but may it not be Dracula anyway!*

"Teasdale!" she cried, arriving at the grove of trees, "where are you?" For strange as it may seem, our poet brother was nowhere to be seen.

"He's vanished!" gasped Leo. "And into thin air!"

"Dracula has him, I know!" sobbed Beth.

"Or Martians!" added Leo.

"Never fear!" cried a voice from above us. "I am still here!"

So we looked up and there was Teasdale, dangling in the

air from a bough by the straps of his knapsack, a good fifteen feet off the ground! Beth didn't know which was the more amazing: how Teasdale managed to get up there or the fact that he hadn't fainted.

It took us a few minutes to figure out how Teasdale had ended up fifteen feet off the ground. Apparently a good-sized bough had been bent down some time previously, perhaps by a large animal landing on it or even a heavy wind, and had become stuck under another bough and remained there, like the string of a bow—taut and just waiting to be released and spring back to its natural position. Leave it to Teasdale to brush against it in his search for some bird and somehow get the straps of his knapsack tangled in it as it went bursting upward in its newfound freedom!

"Really, Teasdale!" laughed Beth once she'd climbed the tree and retrieved him. "That's the second time this summer you've been trapped in a tree!"

"I'd rather you didn't remind me," sniffed the pale poet. "I prefer to have such misadventures behind me!"

"With our luck," teased Beth, "who knows what could happen next!"

"Well, forget it for now," interrupted Leo. "We wasted around ten minutes getting you down! If we stand here yapping, we'll never get back before Mrs. Bell has to drive off to that board meeting!"

Hand in hand in hand we approached the bridge. About a yard from it we paused, so Teasdale could gather courage to cross it.

He took a step forward alone, inspected the bridge for the first time, and then turned back toward us.

"Forget it!" he said. "Crossing that bridge I'll never be, until I start hating poetry!"

"Christopher Columbus!" exclaimed Beth. "We'll hold your hands!"

"Never!" Teasdale stated.

93

"Listen," began Leo, "if you don't—" when all of a sudden Teasdale gave a high-pitched shriek, turned, and ran alone across the bridge like a cat.

"I guess you talked him into it, Leo," commented Beth.

On the far side of the bridge, Teasdale was hopping up and down and waving his arms. His mouth was wide open, as if he were trying to scream but unable to produce a sound.

"Look at him!" laughed Leo. "He must have just figured out what he did!"

Then, from across the bridge, Teasdale called out:

"Quick! run over the bridge to me!
There's something lurking behind that tree!"

"Of all the silly—" began Beth when a twig snapped not far behind us. Then another. And another.

"C'mon, Leo!" cried Beth. "Maybe Teasdale's right!"

So in three seconds flat we were all on the far side of the ravine. We couldn't help but peer back behind us, at a big oak tree Teasdale claimed was hiding somebody—or something.

As we were watching, the ground between the tree and the bridge wriggled, just as though an enormous snake were burrowing there. Then came an odd cracking sound —and the bridge went tumbling to the bottom of the ravine.

In the silence after its fall, Beth swore she heard footsteps retreating back down the mountain.

"Christopher Columbus!" exclaimed Beth. "What happened to the bridge?"

"Beats me," Leo sighed. "But I aim to find out!"

"Hey, Teasdale—how are you doing?" Beth wanted to know, Teasdale having been very silent.

But Teasdale gave no answer—there was no Teasdale.

Our first response was to look up—in case he was dangling from another pine tree. But the only tree nearby had no Teasdale dangling from it. We then examined the long grass at our feet. "I bet he just fainted into the grass!" piped Leo. But he hadn't.

And neither had he had the time to run and hide behind the stone house. "He just couldn't have run that fast!" said Beth. "Especially since the last time I saw him he was standing right near the bridge."

"Right near the what?" said Leo in a low voice.

Beth looked at Leo. Leo looked at Beth. Very slowly we approached the bank of the ravine and very slowly we looked down.

Below us, dangling from one of the broken-off bridge supports by the strap of his knapsack, was Teasdale!

"Oh my God!" gasped Beth. "Teasdale! Are you all right?"

"Tell me I'm dreaming all this or I'll faint again!" came a small voice below us.

"Quick!" cried Beth, "we've got to do something! That knapsack strap can't hold him forever!"

Thank goodness the rope Aunt Henrietta had insisted we bring wasn't in Teasdale's knapsack. And thank goodness the only practical thing in the world Teasdale is good at is tying knots. And thank goodness Beth and Leo are strong and athletic.

Inch by inch we pulled until at last Teasdale's dark head appeared at the rope's end, above the side of the ravine. At last all of him was back on solid ground, and we were able to hug and kiss him and make sure he hadn't been hurt.

While Teasdale lay recovering eating a chocolate bar, Beth checked the stone house and Leo examined where the bridge had been.

"No candle in the window," announced Beth. "So no Dracula, either!"

"And no snake in the grass," said Leo.

"No what in the who?" asked Teasdale.

"Remember, just before the bridge collapsed, that the ground around it was wriggling? Well, it looks like there

95

was a rope attached to the supports of the bridge, and I bet someone pulled on it to send the whole thing flying!"

"It must have been an awfully weak bridge," remarked Beth.

"They sawed the supports a bit first," Leo explained. "Remember, Beth, you kept saying you thought we were being followed? Then when we stopped for our snack, he got ahead of us, fixed up the bridge and the rope—and waited! Then, once we were across the bridge, he made sure we couldn't get back again!"

"But why? And who?" demanded Beth.

"I can tell you the why," Leo answered, looking at Mrs. Bell's map. "With the bridge gone, the only way back to the hotel is a long roundabout route—it will take hours and hours!"

"So?"

"So we'll never get back in time for the board meeting! Don't you get it—someone wants to make sure we're out of the way for the board meeting!" stated Leo.

"You must be right," agreed Beth. "But who would do this? And why?"

"I say Jon," Leo replied. "I just stopped believing in Dracula. I say it's been Jon all along—and he knows we know. So he thinks if we miss the board meeting, Mrs. Bell might not be able to prove it was he. He really must want to see the hotel destroyed!"

"There's only one problem with your theory," Beth replied. "Whoever it was had to follow us up, pass us, saw the bridge, tie the rope, and then hide until we came. I don't think Jon even knew we were coming up here today."

"He could have been listening at the door," suggested Leo. "I still say it's Jon!"

"Hmmm," pondered Beth. "What's your opinion, Teas?"

"Jon's no friend of mine, and I'm no friend of his," began Teasdale, "but Jon the villain? I just don't think he is! Though I don't know why," he added, lapsing out of rhyme.

Beth thought for a moment. "It's gotta be Bill," she said. "Mrs. Bell suspected that Bill wasn't working as hard as he could to figure out what's going on—and if the board decides to keep the hotel open but replace Mrs. Bell, Bill would be the logical replacement for her. He could have dressed up like Dracula and made himself look like Jon at the same time, just to put the blame on Jon! And Bill knew we were coming up here, and remember how he rushed off from Mrs. Bell's office? I bet he was going up to Dead Man's Drop—and with a saw and a rope!"

"Yeah," said Leo. "And it was Bill who showed Mrs. Bell that vampire legend book and told her all about Pine Peak and the cabin and the candle and everything . . ."

"But he was so nice to us," sighed Beth.

"Maybe too nice," said Leo ominously.

"True," agreed Teasdale. "And I'll quote again from Shakespeare if you're willin': 'One can smile and smile and still be a villain.'"

"But Christopher Columbus!" exclaimed Beth. "We've got to get back before the board meeting to tell Mrs. Bell! There's still time for her to solve the mystery and save the hotel!"

"But with the bridge on the ravine floor, the hike'll take many an hour and more!" observed Teasdale mournfully.

"Not while I'm around!" Leo boasted in his serious scientific-type voice. And before our very eyes, using the rope with which we'd rescued Teasdale, plus the yards of bandages Henrietta had packed for us, Leo constructed a rope-swing. He tied it to the big tree overlooking the ravine, the one in which we'd first looked for Teasdale.

"It'll be easy!" Leo told us. "Just step back as far as the rope can go, run forward, and when you get to the ravine, jump up and hold on with all your might!"

"I'll walk back the long way," said Teasdale, eyeing the rope and the ravine.

"No way!" replied Beth. "We stay together!"

It didn't take Beth long to come up with a plan. First she swung herself across the ravine, bellowing like Tarzan as she flew. Then Leo tied Teasdale onto the rope and gave it a mighty push, jumping on for the ride at the last moment. When the rope swung over to the far side, Leo jumped off and Beth was waiting with her Swiss army knife; the idea was that she'd slice through the rope so Teasdale could just tumble to safety.

Part one worked just fine; Teasdale and Leo came swooping over the ravine with Teasdale tied on tight just in case he fainted. On the other side, Leo leaped off gracefully and Beth gave an enormous swing with her knife, cutting the rope.

But not all the way through! As we watched, horrified and helpless, Teasdale went swinging *back* over the ravine, dangling precariously from a few strands of rope!

"Farewell!" he cried as he swung away from us and "Do something!" as he swung back.

We leaped into action. When Teasdale swung back to our side of the ravine, Leo grabbed him to stop him and Beth started sawing frantically with her knife. As the force of the swing's movement started dragging the three of us back toward the ravine's brink, Leo had the sense to keep digging in his heels to slow us down, and Beth had the sense to keep on sawing. At the last second, just when the ravine's floor seemed to be gaping below us, Beth cut through the rope and we all fell in a heap on the ground.

As soon as we found our breath again, and calmed down Teasdale, who uncharacteristically had become hysterical instead of fainting, we practically flew back down the mountain. We couldn't help but imagine the look of gratitude on Mrs. Bell's face when we arrived in time to save the day!

Chapter Twelve

Incredible Information

The hotel was strangely empty. We raced through corridor after vacant corridor and just about the only sound we heard was some typing from Mr. O'Hanrahan's room.

"Everyone can't have checked out!" said Leo as we ran toward Mrs. Bell's private quarters.

"I hope not—at least for Mrs. Bell's sake," Beth replied.

A slight surprise awaited us as we entered the lobby near Mrs. Bell's quarters. There was Aunt Henrietta, emptying the contents of her pill bag into the garbage pail.

"Aunt Henrietta!" gasped Beth. "What are you doing?"

Our aunt looked up, paused for a moment, and said; "You know, children, I've learned a lot of things this afternoon—all very interesting, all very different. Things about others, and things about myself."

"This sounds more than fascinating—so kindly explain without hesitating!" urged Teasdale.

"Wait a second!" ordered Beth. "We've found out a thing or two ourselves—and we've got to tell them to Mrs. Bell right away, before the board meeting!"

"You're in luck, then," our aunt replied. "I just ran into Anna, who'd just run into Mrs. Bell, and she said Mrs. Bell had mentioned the meeting had had to be postponed until early evening—something to do with a new member from New York being delayed, I believe."

"Good," said Beth with a sigh of relief. "I need to catch my breath anyway—we practically ran the whole way back!"

Taking seats around our aunt, we settled back in the lounge to hear our aunt's tale.

"Well," she began, "it goes something like this. I had the busiest and perhaps most exciting afternoon of my entire life—or, I should say, of the last seven years of my life, the seven years since my marriage broke up. And, can you believe it, even though I was dashing around town, tiptoeing down hallways, and mercy knows what else, I didn't feel ill for an instant! And I realized that one big reason I've been sick so much was that it gave me something to do. I mean, everybody gets sick once in a while—but I had something wrong with me all the time. I guess it was just my way of running away. But today, just being so busy, and knowing I was doing something to help not only poor Mrs. Bell, but especially you three—my niece and nephews, the children of my brother and my dear sister-in-law—well, it made me feel like a different person. And I have you children to thank."

Of course we all blushed and felt embarrassed. "Aunt Henrietta," said Beth slowly, "I'm really glad you've found a way to be happier. And I'm sorry we didn't help you more before. We knew you used to be different, but we didn't think enough about it to do anything. I'm sorry."

"Me too," added Teasdale.

"And me three," put in Leo.

"So tell us—what else did you find out?" asked Beth after a moment's silence.

"You won't believe it," replied our aunt, "though it certainly will explain a lot. There was one thing that struck me as being especially suspicious about the two times I saw Jon in town—and it was that just about every time I was in town, and happened to be near the same place—the pharmacy, as it happens—I saw Bill lurking around. And he always looked nervous—just as though he were scared of being seen."

"If you're going to tell us Bill's involved, we've already kind of figured that out," interrupted Leo.

"But how?"

So then we had to stop and tell our aunt about our adventures at Dead Man's Drop. She turned paler and paler as we told our tale. When Beth had finished her narrative, our aunt said:

"Hmmm—they must be getting desperate!"

"Who's 'they'?" demanded Leo.

"That's what I want to tell you," our aunt replied. "Well—after thinking it was odd to see Bill at that spot so many times, I decided to go to town and investigate. I hadn't been there more than five minutes when I lucked out—I saw Frank coming down the street. I scooted behind a tree so he didn't see me and I followed him. For one horrible minute he stopped and I was sure he had spotted me—but he had just run into someone he knew and that was why he stopped. About two minutes away from the town common where I thought I hit Jon, Frank entered quite an attractive-looking apartment building. I trailed him down the hallway and saw him enter a door at the far end of the ground floor. As soon as he had gone in I raced to the door and put my ear up against it to see what I could hear."

"And what did you hear?" we asked excitedly.

"Nothing, I'm afraid. The door was simply too thick. So without wasting a second, I dashed back outside to the alleyway on the side of the building, and again luck was with me. There was a large trash bin and a smaller garbage pail right against the window. So I climbed up on the pail, and leaning for support against the bin, I was able to peek in the window—and wait till you hear what I saw!"

"Tell us!" Leo practically shouted.

"I saw Frank, of course, and I saw who he was talking to. At first I thought it was Jon, and I thought it was no surprise to find Jon mixed up in something sordid. After all, he hasn't been exactly pleasant. But I listened awhile—and it was long enough to get it all figured out. The man Frank was speaking with looked like Jon, sounded like Jon, and acted like Jon—but he *wasn't* Jon!"

101

"I don't think I follow you," said Beth.

"Of course not," our aunt replied. "It was something none of us knew. Jon has a twin brother, Jasper! And all the times when Jon seemed to have been in two places at one time, it's been because he has a twin!"

"They look that much alike?" wondered Leo.

"Like two peas in a pod—except it's Jasper who has the limp. I mean it was he who had the little mishap with my Panhard."

"But is Jon in on it, too?" asked Beth.

"Wait and I'll tell you. From what I could learn, Bill, Frank, and Jasper are in on a scheme to drive Mrs. Bell out of business. They started by making those dreadful screams at night; then when that wasn't scaring away enough customers, they began circulating that Dracula legend—apparently you weren't the only ones they told about it. Finally, they got you kids involved with that camera to photograph the supposed Dracula—thus putting the blame on Jon, who seems to be completely innocent. Although I must say I don't see what Bill and Frank and this Jasper fellow will gain by the hotel going out of business . . ."

"We figured that out," Beth announced. "Bill's counting on the board not to close the hotel, but to replace Mrs. Bell—with him. Then he can get his friends good jobs and probably even start embezzling money! He must have wanted us out of the way during the board meeting so we wouldn't be able to back up Mrs. Bell and to give evidence that it couldn't have been Jon pretending to be Dracula!"

"That poor Mrs. Bell!" sighed our aunt. "I've never been especially drawn to the woman—but no doubt it's because she's had so much on her mind. She probably had an inkling about what was going on."

"Yeah," said Leo. "I remember her saying she thought Bill hadn't done a very careful job, or something like that."

"Right," Beth agreed, "and I bet this explains why Jon's

102

been so grumpy—he must have known they were up to something, but didn't know exactly what. I bet that's why he didn't want us hanging around the farm!"

"Yeah," said Leo yet again. "But there's one thing I don't get. All that stuff about Dracula, well—I mean it turned out not to be true, but it did really come from books and all. Remember Aunt Henrietta read to us from that book Bill gave Mrs. Bell."

"I can explain that," our aunt told us. "I overheard Frank saying to Jasper that it was a good thing Bill had come across those old Dracula legends and that Mrs. Bell had bought the idea—it gave them a good cover."

"Did you hear anything else?" Beth wanted to know.

"Just a bit. I heard Frank telling Jasper that pretty soon they'd be in the money—and I'm pretty sure he mentioned something to do with the decision the board would be making today. Well—it was at this moment I had my mishap. I leaned a bit closer to get a better view of Jasper, lost my balance slightly, and ended up knocking against the window just a touch—but I guess I did make a bit of noise. And I guess Frank and Jasper heard it, because the last thing I heard was Frank saying he thought he heard someone at the window and would go and look. Of course I was frantic—it was a long alleyway with nowhere to hide—so I had no choice."

"You let him see you?" gasped Leo.

"Of course not!" giggled our aunt. "I summoned all my courage and tried hard not to think about all those allergies I used to have—and I dove into the trash bin. I won't even begin to tell you what manner of trash was in it—suffice it to say that when Frank looked out the window, all he saw was a trash bin and a garbage pail. Your aunt was out of sight!"

"Hooray for Henrietta!" we all shouted and cheered loudly.

"Although in garbage you had to dive," said Teasdale with great ceremony, "we think you're the greatest aunt alive!"

* * *

It was at least five minutes later, after we'd finished cheering, and had made our aunt tell us four times in a row what it was like to be buried in garbage, that Beth suddenly said:

"Christopher Columbus! Even if that board meeting was delayed, we'd still better hurry along and tell Mrs. Bell what we've learned!"

"Roger!" agreed Leo.

Aunt Henrietta said that we three kids should go tell Mrs. Bell ourselves—after all, it was we who had risked our lives at Dead Man's Drop to solve the mystery, we should have the fun of telling her.

"And besides," our aunt added, "I'm afraid I had a little mix-up with the Panhard!"

"Aunt Henrietta!" laughed Beth, "whom did you run over this time?"

"I ran over no one," our aunt replied. "It's just that as I was driving back from town, right near the gates of the hotel, I thought I observed an especially unusual wild flower growing in the meadow. On investigating, I found first one flower, then another, then another—and before I knew it, I had picked myself a bouquet and was back at the hotel—but with the Panhard still sitting by the gates. I do hope no one steals it."

"I kind of doubt it," Leo told her, "except maybe a Martian invader who mistook it for a UFO!"

"Well," laughed our aunt, "I'm no Martian invader—but I do happen to like my Panhard. So off I go to pick it up. I'll see you children back here in an hour or two—say around seven o'clock?"

"Fine by us," Beth agreed as we headed off to find Mrs. Bell.

Mrs. Bell wasn't in her private quarters, so we raced down hallway after hallway until we finally located her in her office. The door was open so we entered without knocking. Mrs. Bell had her head bowed over some papers and didn't even see us come in—that's how hard she was concentrating. Beth imagined she must be trying hard to come up with something to say to the board.

"We're back!" shouted Leo as though we'd been gone for three years, not three hours. I guess he must have really shouted extra loud for he seemed to startle Mrs. Bell. She looked up, saw it was us, and gave a little gasp. She was so surprised she dropped the papers she'd been going over.

"Goodness!" she said. "How you surprised me! And back so soon! My, you must be clever hikers," she continued as she quickly picked up the fallen papers.

"We're not just clever hikers," Leo told her. "We're also clever investigators!"

"Whatever are you talking about!" inquired Mrs. Bell.

"Just you wait, Mrs. Bell, till you hear what we have to tell," Teasdale informed her.

"I'm waiting," she replied. "Do go on."

So while Mrs. Bell listened with her mouth open, Beth began her story. She started with the first time we'd heard the screams and was just about to end with our aunt's discoveries when Mrs. Bell interrupted her.

"You certainly are clever children," she said in a quivering voice. "This is absolutely—amazing. You've made simply marvelous detectives. I don't know quite what to say!"

"Oh, it was nothing," Beth said modestly.

"But, you know," put in Leo, "as I listened to Beth repeat the entire story, I thought of a few things."

"Such as?" Mrs. Bell asked quietly.

"Well—such as we should have known all along there was no Dracula. I hate to say it but Beth was right. And we should have guessed Bill and Frank were in on it. I mean, Frank almost led us to Rose's body—he told us where to go strawberry hunting. And it was Bill who told us the old legends first to make us want to investigate. And it was Bill too who sort

105

of talked us into trying to photograph Dracula—I mean so you wouldn't blame him for everything that was going wrong. And that way he got evidence against Jon, but without having to get it himself, which might have seemed suspicious."

"Right!" agreed Beth. "And it was Bill who showed Mrs. Bell the *Vampir Legende* book!"

"But there's more," went on Leo. "Remember the cow we thought we saw get killed by Dracula?"

"How could we forget?" asked Beth.

"Well," said Leo, "we should have been smart enough to realize that the blood around the supposed neck wound wouldn't have scabbed up so quickly. When we got there a second after it happened it already was dry! We should have known from what the doctor said when our aunt hurt her elbow—that bleeding wounds take at least five minutes to scab up. And also remember Teasdale touched the cow, and she already was cold! That means she must have been killed hours before and they just had her waiting there till we showed up!"

"But what about those screams?" Beth wondered.

"Remember that wire Teasdale tripped over? They must have had a loudspeaker hidden somewhere! And they just kept broadcasting recordings of screams until someone started investigating! And that's not all!"

"That's for sure!" agreed Beth. "Just wait till you hear what our aunt—"

"I've heard quite enough already!" interrupted Mrs. Bell. "I can't believe my men would do this to me! You'll just have to save the rest of your information for the police! I'll have to call them immediately. Let's see . . . the board meeting is now scheduled to start at seven-thirty; it's a forty-minute drive to the lawyer's office in Parkersville—I'll have to call the police straight away. Perhaps I can get this all, um, cleared up by the time I have to leave for the meeting."

"Great!" cheered Beth. "I bet we've saved the hotel!"

106

"Uh, yes," replied Mrs. Bell. "I—I just can't get it all straight in my head! But call the police I must!"

Mrs. Bell picked up the phone and dialed. She asked to speak to the captain and proceeded to tell him everything. We three kids couldn't help but swell with pride as Mrs. Bell told him all we'd done and discovered.

"Boy!" said Leo when Mrs. Bell had hung up. "What would you have done without us?"

"I'm, ah, sure I don't know," she replied, in a very distracted voice. "I really hate doing this," she muttered half to herself.

"Doing what!" we wondered.

"Why, um, turning in Bill and Frank—they've been with me for years!"

"Oh, Mrs. Bell," said Beth, "you're an old softy! Feeling sorry for them after what they did to you!"

"Listen," added Leo, "could we stay and talk with the police, too? I've always wanted to be interrogated as a witness! Can we, Mrs. Bell?"

"Call me Odelia," Mrs. Bell responded. "And of course you can stay. In fact, the captain specifically asked you to be here so he could question you without delay. I have an idea—I'll call out to the kitchen to bring us a little something while we're waiting."

We were waiting at least ten minutes after Mrs. Bell called the kitchen, and Leo's stomach was rumbling so loudly it was starting to get embarrassing when at last there was a knock on the door.

Beth wondered who it was—the waiter with a snack or the police come to question us. It turned out to be neither. It was instead the last people on earth we were expecting to see!

Chapter Thirteen
Cold Comfort

"What are you doing here?" gasped Beth as Bill, Frank, and Jasper entered Mrs. Bell's office. It was amazing how exactly Jasper resembled Jon—but his expression was different enough for us to tell which twin it was.

Bill's only answer was a horrible smirk, after which he locked the door behind him and leaned up against it. He gave his blond hair a shake and laughed. Frank had crossed the office and was sitting on Mrs. Bell's desk, leafing through the papers she'd been reading when we'd entered.

It was Jasper who spoke first. He looked at us with interest. "So these are the kids who've been so clever. Too bad for them!"

"Children," interrupted Mrs. Bell, "meet Jasper—Jon's twin brother!"

"W-what's going on here?" demanded Beth. "And where are the police?"

"And where's our snack?" wondered Leo.

"Snack!" mocked Bill. "Odelia—haven't you told them yet?"

"Of course not!" snapped Mrs. Bell. "If they'd found out the real truth before you three got here, I might not have been able to keep them here myself—and that would have spoiled the whole thing. We have to move fast—I have to leave soon for the board meeting and I want these three out of the way by then. They outsmarted us at Dead Man's Drop by building that swing—this time we'll make sure they can't be so clever! I'll tell you what to do, but I'd rather not be around to see it!"

"See what?" shouted Leo. "You might at least tell us what's going on around here! And where are the cops? Why aren't they here yet?"

"I don't think you really want to know," began Beth softly. All of a sudden she knew how a fly in a spider's web feels. "Leo—" she started when Mrs. Bell interrupted.

"It's like this," she said, "the police aren't coming—at least not until later—when they come for Jon!"

"B-but—we heard you call them!" cried Leo.

"On the contrary. You heard me speak into the phone and presumed I was speaking to the police. Actually, I was speaking to Bill, letting him know the plan at Dead Man's Drop hadn't worked."

Leo's mouth fell open and he gave a huge gasp. "But that means . . . that means . . ."

"Quite right, my dear," answered Mrs. Bell. "You seem at last to have figured it out. Yes—it was all as you thought: Bill and Frank—and of course Jasper, whom you just met— *were* involved in a scheme to ruin Hidden Mountain Health Hotel. You only overlooked one little thing: It was *I* who was the mastermind! *I* who was directing each and every move!"

"Christopher Columbus!" Beth exclaimed. "We should have known something was fishy about you, the way you kept encouraging us to investigate! You even started the whole thing by sending us to the farm with a message for Bill the day the phones weren't working."

"But they *were* working!" Leo chimed in. "Remember? Jon was on the phone when we were loading Teasdale into the car that day after we found Rose. Why didn't we think of that before!"

"But why?" Beth asked Mrs. Bell. "Why would you want to ruin your own hotel?"

"C'mon, Odelia," sneered Bill. "Tell 'em the whole story. No one will listen to a bunch of crazy kids anyway!"

109

"Why not?" Mrs. Bell replied. "They might as well know what's going on. You see," she continued, now talking to us, "while I make a decent living running this hotel, it certainly is a lot of hard work. And since I'm not getting any younger, I decided there must be a better way. It was Bill who suggested selling this land for development—you know, housing projects, condominiums, shopping centers—whatever. As you might well imagine, two thousand acres would go for a pretty penny—six million dollars, to be exact. But there was one little problem: my husband's will. In it the old fool left a codicil saying that the hotel and the land surrounding it could be sold for development only if the hotel lost money two years running, and the board felt it would be impossible to recover the losses in the third year. Well, as I've already mentioned to you, last year we were lucky with the weather: It rained virtually nonstop from May to October. Nice for the reservoirs and nice for me: We lost barrels of money—after all, who wants to go to the mountains in the rain?"

"I do!" proclaimed Teasdale. "Mountains in the rain are soft and sweet; to hike among them is really a—"

"Cut the culture, kid!" Bill interjected rudely. "Let Odelia finish!"

"Well," continued Mrs. Bell, "it was my clever friend Bill who discovered a way to ensure we'd lose money this year. He came across the Dracula legend you children found so fascinating. We started slowly—with just the screams at first. Then when you children happened along we got lucky again—that old cow named Rose happened to die, so we made those marks on her neck and arranged for you to find her, and started you off thinking about Dracula! We knew a vampire scare would send all the guests packing. The only problem was it might be pinned on us. Then we came up with Jasper. We got Jasper to impersonate Jon pretending to be Dracula. I gave Jon the motive to do such a thing when I gave him his notice—so if we got investigated, they'd think he was doing it all as revenge. And I'm positive we'll be able to convince the board that Jon and the Dracula legend which you dear children helped so much to spread with all your energetic investigating have damaged the hotel irreparably. I am sure that at the meeting they'll agree to let me sell—especially since I promised three of the six board members percentages of the six million we'll get. You see, while the board can stop me from selling, the land is mine—each last acre! I can't wait to wash my hands of this old dump!"

"But it's beautiful land!" argued Beth. "And anyway, Jon'll be able to say it wasn't he being Dracula and the police'll prove it was Jasper in around thirty seconds flat!"

"Yeah!" agreed Leo. "And if the police don't believe Jon, they'll believe Mrs. Fillipelli! *She* saw Jon in the kitchen when you'll say he was out in the barnyard being Dracula!"

"We are not nearly as foolish as you might think us, you dear children," replied Mrs. Bell. "We have considered all this and acted accordingly. Tell them what we've been up to, Bill—aside from sawing the supports on the bridge! That much they already know!"

"It's like this," said Bill. "As for Mrs. Fillipelli, not that anyone would ever *really* listen to anything that hippo said—but just in case, we sent her home early. In fact, she's already gone."

"What do you mean 'sent her home'?" asked Beth.

"It was easy," Bill explained. "We sent her a fake telegram from her husband, telling her he was coming home early—tonight, in fact. Then we sent a cab to pick her up and take her to the airport—all timed so she'd be gone way before the board meeting—and that was even before they postponed it! So she and her information are out of our hair. And to be extra clever, we sent a follow-up telegram, saying the first one was a mistake—just in case we were questioned

111

about it later—we could say it had all been a mistake! Too bad it arrived after we'd called the taxi!"

"And what about our aunt?" demanded Beth. "She saw Jasper in town when you say Jon was on the farm—that'll prove Jon has a twin and he was involved!"

"Oh really, Beth," mocked Mrs. Bell. "Do you honestly believe any jury in the world would listen to your aunt? She's such a confused creature, I imagine if they even asked her her last name, she'd have an allergy attack!"

"Our aunt's smarter than that!" boasted Leo. "And that's not all she knows!"

"What exactly do you mean by that?" Mrs. Bell said in an icy voice.

"Our aunt—" Leo began when a quick kick from Beth on one side and Teasdale on the other silenced him. I guess we both felt the less Mrs. Bell knew about our aunt's discoveries the better.

"Yes?" said Mrs. Bell.

"She, um, she, why, she knows all about Panhards and other French cars like Citroëns and Facel-Vegas!"

"Really!" snorted Mrs. Bell. "Your aunt's knowledge of her hideous car and others like it is of no interest to me!"

"But why'd you try to trap us up on Dead Man's Drop?" demanded Leo.

"Simple," Mrs. Bell replied. "You three seemed to be narrowing in on the truth—that Jon simply couldn't have been in all those places at once. I felt it was just a matter of time before you figured out there had to be someone else involved. And once you got that far, it wouldn't have been too hard to figure out I was in on it too! And I just couldn't risk you showing up at the board meeting and opening up your big mouths! So I decided to get you out of the way until the board meeting was over."

"But what about Jon?" Beth wanted to find out. "He'll just tell everybody he has a twin!"

112

"Had a twin," Mrs. Bell responded simply.

"Had a twin?" we asked.

"Yes—had," she replied. "You see, Jasper has been living in Canada these past few years. And one of his friends just happens to work for the Montreal coroner's office—and he arranged a phony death certificate for Jasper—as of seven months ago, in fact. So should Jon start babbling about some twin, why when they investigate they'll find this twin died over half a year ago. They'll think Jon's crazy!"

"Not if we go get him right away, and bring him to the meeting!" challenged Leo.

"That's not very likely," sneered Mrs. Bell. "Tell 'em all about it, Jasper!"

"You know my brother—he always likes doing things regular-like. Gets up at the same time, goes to the bed at the same time. So, what he does every evening, starting around six, is to climb up to the top of the silo and sit and read. You know the place—the one with the rickety ladder. So, after he'd gone up, I quietly sneaked up and bolted the door behind him. Even if he climbs down before night, he'll never get out till someone goes and lets him out."

"You—you'd betray your own brother?" Beth asked Jasper.

"Why not?" he replied. "The price is right."

"Yes," smiled Mrs. Bell, "by the time Jon gets out of the barn, the board meeting will be long over, and Jasper will be out of the country. After all, Canada's not far from here. And besides, he's dead anyway—who'd bother looking for him?"

"But we'll tell!" said Beth. "You can't stop us!"

"I can't, can't I?" Mrs. Bell purred. "In the long run, no—I'm sure you children will shoot your mouths off. But who shall believe you? I've already noted what imaginative little beings you are—so sure about Dracula and UFOs and princes on the hillside! Not a soul will believe you. And

113

by then it would be too late anyway—I am quite sure the board will decide as I hope they will. And once they sign the paper tonight, it'll be too late. I have a developer all lined up—his bulldozers all oiled and ready for action. And once the papers are signed closing the hotel, the board is dissolved immediately! It'll all be mine, mine, mine—and with no strings attached!"

"Then we'll go to the meeting ourselves!" Leo told her.

"Sorry, dear, but I have other other plans for you. The three of you will be spending the evening in the freezer. It should be a bit chilly, but you won't freeze—we've turned the temperature up a shade. And you won't suffocate either—we've turned the ventilator fan on."

"But how will you explain our just happening to be in the freezer?" demanded Beth.

"I imagine I'll say you three dear children were in search of some goodies to eat and the door happened to swing shut behind you! What a dreadful pity you won't be discovered until tomorrow morning, after the meeting is over and the board members have left!" Mrs. Bell replied.

"Then our aunt will wonder where we are!" said Beth. "She'll come look for us!"

"We'll just send her one of our fake notes" was the grim response. "This may be cold comfort, but before you, ah, visit the freezer, shall we say, I'd like to thank you so much, dear children, for all you've done, especially the photo of Dracula. And if it's of any consolation, both those cows died of natural causes—my, wasn't that good timing! And speaking of timing—I have a meeting to attend. And you have an appointment in the kitchen. Take 'em away, boys—and be quick about it!"

We put up quite a fight—even Teasdale. Beth broke loose from Jasper and managed to kick Mrs. Bell around fourteen times on the shins and punch her a few times in the belly before Jasper got her with some sort of karate chop that would have floored Godzilla. It sent Beth flying across the room where she landed with a crash and twisted her ankle painfully. Leo meanwhile had leaped out of Bill's grasp and had crawled under Mrs. Bell's desk where the crooks couldn't find him—at least for a while. And when they finally discovered where he was, he sure gave them a run for their money. I've never seen anybody move so fast; his arms and legs were one big blur—a little like those photographs of hummingbirds they're always showing you in science class. He must have given Bill a lot of sharp kicks and punches—Bill kept groaning and cursing. And Teasdale, who I don't think had ever fought before in his entire life, did a good job on Frank. He grabbed hold of Frank's curly hair and pulled mightily, at the same time biting Frank on the chin. In fact, Teasdale bit him so hard he started to bleed and even let go of Teasdale, who dashed to the door, which unfortunately was locked.

All our efforts were in vain. In less than five minutes our rebellion was quelled and we were dragged down to the kitchen, screaming and struggling the whole way. Mrs. Bell had to come along and assist Frank with Teasdale—he seemed to be struggling the hardest. Leo and Beth were yelling things like "Help!" and "Let go!" and a few swear words I'd rather not mention. Teasdale was shouting things like "Unhand me, you villain!" and "Let me loose, you ugly goose!" but nobody came to our rescue.

The only funny thing that happened was that in his struggles Teasdale pulled hard at Mrs. Bell's bun—and it came off! It turned out she wore a hairpiece, so her bun was a fake—just the way she was.

But it wasn't funny enough to make us laugh—especially after we'd been forced into the giant freezer and had the door slammed shut behind us!

* * *

115

Despite what Mrs. Bell had said about raising the temperature, it was unbelievably cold in that freezer—in less than two minutes our toes and fingers were numb and our teeth chattering.

We screamed and shouted and knocked madly on the walls. It was no good. No one could hear us, and there was absolutely no way out from the inside. I think it would be easier to break into Fort Knox. Beth swore if she ever got out she'd never again go near another freezer as long as she lived. She'd even give up all frozen foods—even ice cream.

For a while we gathered by the ventilator fan—the small bit of fresh air that it propelled into the freezer wasn't nearly so stale as the rest of the air around us. We also knew that without this input of fresh air we would gradually suffocate—and somehow its tiny whirring sound seemed friendly.

Leo reminded us that we'd stay warmer for longer if we kept on moving, so we did. With Beth leaning on her brothers' shoulders because of her twisted ankle, we circled the huge freezer, walking in the dim light among boxes and boxes of frozen food.

It took us a minute or two to notice the difference, perhaps because we were so busy walking.

"Something's different," Leo observed, peering around in the faint light.

"What do you mean?" asked Beth.

"I don't know" was the response, "but something's different."

Beth looked around too. Then her jaw dropped and her expression changed.

"Christopher Columbus!" she groaned. "The ventilator fan's stopped working!"

We dashed over—and Beth was right.

"It must have shorted-circuited," Leo told us grimly.

"W-what does this mean?" asked Teasdale.

"It means no more fresh air," Leo replied. "And I think

116

it means it'll keep getting colder and colder—the fresh air coming in was a bit warmer than the rest of the air in this place!"

We all draped ourselves around each other to preserve body heat and kept on circling around the dark freezer, trying to breathe deep but a bit more slowly than usual—to preserve oxygen.

"I can't stand the smell of this place," moaned Leo twenty minutes later as we made our seventieth circle around our prison.

"I can hardly breathe!" gasped Beth.

"It's so cold!" said Teasdale and started to cry.

"Just keep walking," comforted Beth. "If we only keep walking we'll be all right—I know we will!"

"Yeah," said Leo slowly as we rounded the corner near where the frozen french fries were stacked, Beth still walking in the middle, between her two brothers.

"Just keep it up, Teas," Beth continued. "Fight like you fought out there when you pulled off dumb Bell's bun!"

Teasdale's only answer was a soft moan, after which he turned ashen, looked at us in panic, his eyes beseeching us helplessly. He then tried to speak but his lips were too cold to form words. Then he fell to the cold freezer floor.

"I don't think he's fainted—I think he's unconscious!" said Beth as she knelt by her fallen brother. "It's this awful cold! And no fresh air! I can't stand it!"

Leo didn't respond. He too gave a small sigh and just seemed to give up. He fell to the floor and curled up and wouldn't speak or answer in any way no matter how hard Beth shook him. All he would do would be to occasionally mutter, "Cold, too cold!"

Teasdale was even worse; he was entirely curled up and completely silent. The scary thing was that his eyes were still open. Beth reached out with a frozen hand to feel if his heart were still beating. It was, but very slowly.

So this is it, thought Beth to herself. *This is how it feels to die.* She started to cry, and leaning up against Teasdale's still body she lay quietly and gradually felt all her body's warmth seeping from her. It was too cold to fight against it anymore—too cold.

Beth looked once at Teasdale's still pale face, strangely lovely in the freezer's half-light, and then saw no more.

Chapter Fourteen

Panhard to Parkersville

It was like a dream. A slanting ray of bright light shot across the dim freezer and the sound of a loud voice speaking echoed in the silence. From somewhere a touch of warm air appeared, like the first day of spring. A voice kept on speaking, though to no one—on and on, not making sense, yet nice to hear.

"Where is it?" it was saying, "I know there was some left. Now, where could it be?"

Footsteps were approaching and the light was still shining in. Beth vaguely felt the slight warmth in the air, but felt it without really feeling or really reacting.

"It's got to be here," said the voice. "Or did I finish it off last night? I can't wait . . . But it's so dark in here . . . No—none here . . ."

Then the footsteps slowly receded toward the door. Beth tried hard to call out, to move, to do something—but in vain.

Unable to react, she watched the large figure move in the light and close the door as it left.

"Mother . . ." Beth murmured to herself when she was dimly aware of the door opening again and the same voice saying, "I better check those boxes in the far corner—maybe that's where it is." Then came the same heavy footsteps slowly approaching—and then an earth-rending shriek that didn't seem to stop, that grew louder and louder and echoed and reechoed in the freezer.

Then there was someone shaking her and shaking her—

but she was still too asleep, too frozen to respond—too cold, too cold.

"Beth! Beth! What are you doing here? Beth!"

Then there were strong arms around her and she was dragged along the freezer floor—out into the light and the warmth and the real air. From out of a half-opened eye, Beth saw a large form reenter the freezer and reappear, first dragging out Teasdale and then Leo.

"Pray God I'm in time!" said the voice which Beth finally recognized as that of Mrs. Fillipelli. Then warm strong hands began vigorously rubbing her and she felt herself cradled against a warm breast.

"No," Beth could just groan. Summoning all her energy, Beth said, "I'm OK; I'm OK—Teasdale went first—make sure he's OK—help Teasdale . . ."

Then Beth passed out.

When Beth came to she saw Mrs. Fillipelli standing in her huge slip and an enormous bra. Her red woolen skirt was draped around Teasdale, her purple sweater with the white reindeer was engulfing Leo, and her blue corduroy shirt was buttoned around Beth's still shivering frame.

Mrs. Fillipelli was heating something on the stove, and she had the gas ovens on with the doors open so the kitchen was like a furnace. Sweat was rolling off her brow as she appeared moments later with three mugs of warm milk and honey.

"Are my brothers all right?" asked Beth after a sip of milk had thawed her frozen lips.

"Honey, they're just fine" was Mrs. Fillipelli's reassuring reply. "Once you all warm up completely and breathe in enough good oxygen there'll be no harm done. Though land sakes alive, it was one close call—your aunt will keel over when she hears about it."

"I've got to get to her—it's important . . ." began Beth

and tried to stand—but her legs were still too weak and her ankle still hurt so she collapsed on the floor.

"Now, now, dear," soothed Mrs. Fillipelli. "In a second or two I'll run up to your rooms and leave your aunt a message."

At this moment Leo stirred to life and looked around him in confusion.

"W-what happened?" he muttered.

"That's just what I've been wanting to ask you—" began Mrs. Fillipelli when Teasdale too revived. Like Leo he looked around him in wonder, but then Beth saw the light of memory shine in his eyes and as she watched, the blue eyes filled with tears and Teasdale began weeping quietly as the horror of the situation returned to him.

"Teasdale . . ." murmured Beth from across the kitchen.

"Save your strength, honey," interrupted Mrs. Fillipelli. "Once you've all finished your milk and honey you can tell me all about it."

"I don't believe it!" said a stunned Mrs. Fillipelli a few minutes later when Beth had finished her explanation. "But I guess I do . . . Imagine that—that old bag stuffing innocent children into a freezer just to make a lousy buck! Wait till I get my hands on her! I didn't win Sicily's Heavyweight Lady's Boxing Championship for nothing! Ooh—and sending me that fake telegram! I was so worried about my little Luigi I almost skipped dessert!"

"Wait a minute!" interrupted Leo. "If you got the telegram how come you're still here?"

Mrs. Fillipelli looked a bit embarrassed. "They sent a taxi to pick me up and drive me to the airport," she replied, "and it was one of those newfangled compacts. And I just couldn't fit in it! And while I was arranging for someone with a larger car to drive me, the second telegram arrived. That's why!"

"Listen," said Beth, "we've got to get busy! That board meeting'll be beginning any second now! We've got to get there and tell them what's happening around here!"

"But what if they don't believe us?" Leo wondered.

"Oh but they will!" said Beth confidently.

"Why?"

"When Mrs. Dumb Bell confesses, that'll make 'em believe us!" replied Beth.

"Huh?" said Leo. "What do you mean?"

"You'll see," Beth answered. "What we have to do now is find Aunt Henrietta so she can drive us to the meeting—remember it's about thirty miles from here—and also to find Jon so he can come with us. You see, my whole plan depends on Jon—and a tape recorder!"

"I have a tape recorder in my room," reported Mrs. Fillipelli, "and finding your aunt shouldn't be hard—we'll just call her room."

There being no answer from our suite, Mrs. Fillipelli tried the front desk, just in case our aunt had left a message.

It turned out she had—a most mysterious message giving an unfamiliar local phone number and the urgent request to call it immediately.

"Town jail," said the voice on the other end of the phone after we'd dialed the number.

"Town what?" exclaimed Beth. "I must have the wrong number!"

"To whom do you wish to speak?" asked the voice.

"Well, um, I was wanting to talk with my Aunt Henrietta," began Beth. "But this must be the wrong num—"

"Oh yeah—the crazy dame with the funny-looking car. You've got the right number. Hold on a moment, please."

"Hello, Beth?" came Aunt Henrietta's voice a minute later. "Listen, Beth dear, I'm afraid I've landed in a tiny bit of trouble!"

"But how? And what? And when? And where?" wondered Beth.

"Well, I went off to retrieve the Panhard and after I did I thought I'd take a little drive. And then I thought I saw a jack-in-the-pulpit—"

"Jack who?"

"Jack-in-the-pulpit, dear—it's a kind of plant. So I drove over to take a look."

"So what's wrong with that?"

"Well," continued Henrietta, "it meant I was driving on the wrong side of the road—though only for an instant, mind you. Was it my fault the town sheriff happened to be driving along that very moment and was forced off the road and ended up careening into a small pond? I say it was most careless of him—I'm sure it disturbed the frogs and lily pads no end! At any rate, they dragged me off to jail and impounded the Panhard until I can pay bail. That's why I called. I don't suppose you have any money on you?"

"About three dollars," replied Beth. "Is that enough?"

"Not by a long shot. I have to pay expenses for removing the sheriff's car from the pond and fixing it, not to mention damage to the police station."

"Damage to the what?" gasped Beth.

"Well, dear, when I drove into town I was so upset that when I arrived at the police station I neglected to stop. It's such a good thing Panhards are made with extra-strength steel—there's hardly a scratch on it!"

"And the police staion?" Beth demanded.

"I'm afraid they'll need a new wall."

"But why didn't you call Dad?" asked Beth. "He's the one with all the money!"

"Oh, dear," replied our aunt. "I should have thought of that. Now it's too late—I'm only allowed the one phone call. Couldn't you ask Mrs. Bell to lend you the money?"

"Christopher Columbus—do you have a lot to hear about!"

123

Beth told her. "But don't worry—we'll get you out, and the Panhard, too! And in a hurry—there's an emergency going on around here! I'll figure out a way—so hold on tight!"

It wasn't hard to figure out a way after all: Mrs. Fillipelli said her pocketbook was stuffed with money—"In case I have to stop for emergency groceries," she explained. And luckily the jail was located in the small town just down the road from the hotel.

"Somebody'll have to get this money down to the jail," announced Beth. "I guess by bicycle would be the best way."

We knew Mrs. Fillipelli would never fit on a bicycle, and since Teasdale doesn't know how to ride one, it would have to be Beth or Leo.

"I'll do it on one of the hotel bikes," volunteered Leo. "It's downhill most of the way—it won't take more than a few minutes!"

"Fine," agreed Beth. "I'll go get Jon, and Teasdale and Mrs. Fillipelli can pick up her tape recorder and wait out front till Leo and Henrietta show up—then we'll all go to that board meeting and show 'em who's boss!"

The moment after Leo had taken Mrs. Fillipelli's handbag and dashed off, Beth went to leave also.

A nasty surprise, however, was in store for Beth when she tried to leave; her ankle was much too painful to put any weight on!

"It must be sprained from when I landed on it up in Mrs. Bell's office," explained Beth sadly. "I could never make it all the way to the farm in time!"

Then came the realization that Teasdale was the only one among us who could go get Jon: Leo had left for town, Beth couldn't go anywhere, and Mrs. Fillipelli, though she could find her way to the silo where Jon was imprisoned, would never be able to climb up the tall rickety ladder. It was only attached by thin little nails to the walls of the silo—Mrs. Fillipelli's massive weight would make the whole thing collapse!

Teasdale turned the color of slush when he heard about the seventy-foot climb, and for a moment Beth was positive he'd faint right then and there, or somewhere on the way to the farm—or, worst of all, halfway up the ladder!

"Teasdale," asked Beth anxiously, "can you do it?"

"I must admit I'm filled with doubt," he answered slowly, "but there's only one way to find out!"

Beth told Teasdale to tell Jon to meet her and Mrs. Fillipelli out front. "Tell him it's vital, if he doesn't want to end up in jail!" she added, and then kissed her brother on both cheeks and wished him luck.

Teasdale soon was nearing the farm. Later he recounted for me his adventures. The first was that on his way there he saw Bill approaching him on the path, a dim but menacing figure in the pale evening light. Upon seeing Bill, Teasdale dove into the long grass lining that part of his route—but too late. Bill had seen something moving and stopped to see what it was.

"Who goes there?" he bellowed in his fake friendly voice. "I know I saw something!"

Teasdale explained that on the spot he made up a small rhyme which gave him strength, and if any of you think poetry is useless, this should prove otherwise.

What Teasdale said to himself was:

> "Don't faint! Stay true!
> You *can* do what you have to do!"

And as that awful Bill began poking around in the long grass, Teasdale gathered all his courage—and miaowed. Nobody can do a better cat imitation than Teasdale. He's been able to do it since he was four and Beth can remember our mom saying it was because Teasdale was part cat.

"It's just a cat," said Bill to himself, continuing on his way.

Once he got to the farm, Teasdale found his way to the large silo. After unbolting the door, he entered and stood inside in speechless horror, gazing at the tall structure and the wobbly ladder scaling its mountainous height.

At first Teasdale tried calling, but his birdlike voice was lost in all the grain—and certainly couldn't be heard by Jon far off at the top, at least five stories away.

Gingerly, Teasdale started climbing. At about fifteen feet off the ground his entire body began shaking and he could hardly breathe. His knees felt like Jell-O and his arms and legs seemed paralyzed. He felt dizzy and very ill—that's how scared by heights he is!

Teasdale clung to the ladder until the first wave of dizziness passed. And then, just as he was sure he was going to faint, Teasdale repeated to himself:

"Don't faint! Stay true!
You *can* do what you have to do!"

Inch by inch and foot by foot Teasdale slowly climbed the seventy-foot ladder. Every few feet he would stop and repeat his rhyme, all the while trying not to think about falling.

At fifty feet Teasdale suffered another dizzy spell, but kept himself going with the help of his rhyme.

Jon meanwhile was sitting comfortably at the silo's top, admiring the sunset, when a pale boy suddenly appeared at the top of the ladder and sprawled out exhausted on the floor of the little loft area that was Jon's private perch.

Jon watched in wonder as Teasdale looked him straight in the eye and said:

126

      "Don't faint! Stay true!
      You *can* do what you have to do!"

"What the—" began Jon when Teasdale burst into tears and sobbed out the entire story.

Once Jon had made sense of what Teasdale had been sobbing, he took Teasdale tenderly in his strong arms and hugged him gently.

"Thank you," said Jon quietly and brushed a tear from Teasdale's cheek.

"I did it! I did it!" sobbed Teasdale. "I made it! And I didn't faint!"

"Teasdale," said Jon, "you're quite a kid."

More tears were shed when Teasdale and Jon joined Mrs. Fillipelli, Beth, Leo, and a just-bailed-out Aunt Henrietta in front of the hotel. Our aunt smothered us in wet tear-drenched kisses when she heard what had happened in the freezer.

When the tears and hugs and crying had subsided, Beth revealed the plan which she and Mrs. Fillipelli had perfected in their absence.

"I've got my tape recorder all ready!" Mrs. Fillipelli told us. "So are we all ready and willing?"

"Of course I'll do it!" said Jon after Beth had explained her plan to him. "It'll provide unbreakable evidence against that Bell monster—and her companions." Then he added more softly, "My brother included."

Teasdale patted Jon consolingly on the shoulder, and Jon turned to us and said:

"I sure owe you an apology. You can probably guess what I'm about to say. I *did* have an inkling about what was going on, though I didn't know my brother was involved. But I knew something was up—and that was why I didn't want you three hanging around the farm. I was scared you might come to harm in some way—as you darn near did tonight. But I guess I could have been nicer about it—you seemed like good kids, but I was too upset to think straight!"

"Don't worry 'bout what's done and past," Teasdale reassured him; "let's just be glad we're friends at last!"

"Well put, Shelley," said Jon, which not only showed what a nice person he really was but that he also knew something about poetry.

Luckily Jon knew how to get to Parkersville, and Henrietta covered the thirty miles to the lawyer's office at a breakneck pace. Beth could tell by the frightened look on Mrs. Fillipelli's broad face that she was wishing Henrietta's Panhard hadn't proved large enough to accommodate her sizable bulk.

At seventy miles per hour, Henrietta careened into the parking lot beside the lawyer's office.

"Hit the brakes, Henrietta!" we shrieked, but too late—with a horrible crunch the Panhard went smashing into a gray Toyota, demolishing its front end completely.

"Oh dear!" commented Henrietta. "This is proving rather an expensive day!"

"I wouldn't worry," chuckled Jon. "That Toyota belongs to Mrs. Bell!"

"Good aim!" cheered Leo as we piled out of the miraculously unscratched Panhard—and headed off to capture Mrs. Bell!

Chapter Fifteen

The Mystery Member

Quietly we entered the lawyer's office. It turned out to be in a suite, with a number of sitting rooms, a secretary's office, a meeting room, and another room or so.

Teasdale, at Beth's direction, entered a lounge and hid behind a sofa, clutching Mrs. Fillipelli's tape recorder.

"Remember, Jon," he said as he slid behind the sofa, "if you have to get up and walk around for some reason, be sure to limp!" In the urgency of the moment he even forgot to rhyme.

Beth, Leo, and Mrs. Fillipelli meanwhile stationed ourselves behind some draperies in the corridor leading to the room where Teasdale was hidden—just in case Jasper appeared we could somehow stop him. It wasn't easy hiding Mrs. Fillipelli behind drapes; Leo later described it as like hiding a tank under a dish towel. But luckily the lights were dim in the corridor so the drapery served its purpose.

"Jasper, what is it?" asked Mrs. Bell irritably. "What are you doing here anyway?"

"It's about Jon," said the real Jon, "and it's urgent!"

"So what is it?" demanded Mrs. Bell. "And hurry up! The meeting is just about to begin—the new member showed up from New York and is freshening up. He should be here soon."

"We can't talk here," said Jon, "someone might overhear us. Follow me to one of the lounges."

"So what is it?" snapped Mrs. Bell as she sat on the sofa.

"It's Jon," repeated Jon. "We thought we'd locked him

in the silo, but he wasn't there! I think he's on to us—I'm afraid he'll show up here and ruin the whole scheme!"

"No!" said Mrs. Bell angrily. "We've gone too far to have him ruin things now! After all our work getting people talking about that legend, setting up those cows so those bothersome brats could find them—not to mention Bill sawing apart that bridge and having to stuff the brats into the freezer! Find out where your brother is and stop him! Remember we're talking about six million dollars!"

At the same moment Mrs. Bell was spilling out the entire story onto the tape recorder Teasdale was holding beneath the sofa, Mrs. Fillipelli, Beth, and Leo were waiting silently behind the drapery.

Leo said he was beginning to think they wouldn't be needed when footsteps sounded down the corridor and we heard a voice saying:

"Yuh, Jasper—I just saw her. She's in the lounge down there."

It was Bill—directing Jasper!

The moment Jasper's sturdy frame passed the drapes, Mrs. Fillipelli sprung into action. Beth thinks that an army of Mrs. Fillipellis could win any war.

What she did was charge right into Jasper, bashing against him with the full force of her nearly three hundred pounds, and knock him flat on the floor. Before he could regain his feet, she leaped on him, landing with a thud on his back, where she stayed smiling. I think it would have taken a bulldozer to have removed Mrs. Fillipelli before she was willing.

"Get off!" groaned the nearly squashed Jasper.

"Scoundrel!" bellowed Mrs. Fillipelli. "Put innocent kids in the freezer, would you? Tell me lies about Luigi, would you?" she asked, bouncing up and down a few times for emphasis.

"I give up! I give up!" moaned the unhappy Jasper.

Mrs. Bell had meanwhile just finished her boastful account of her criminal activities by saying:

"Well—no doubt that board member is ready now. You take care of Jon, and in less than an hour, you and I will be millionaires—won't we, Jasper?"

"I'm not Jasper," said Jon in a low voice.

"Whatever do you mean?" asked Mrs. Bell, getting to her feet and reaching slowly into her purse.

"I said I'm not Jasper. The game's up, Bell—we've got all this on tape. I'm Jon, and I'm going to turn you in. So c'mon!"

"Not so fast!" Mrs. Bell replied, pulling a small hand pistol out of her purse. "Guns come in so handy!" she purred as she took a step closer to where Jon was still sitting on the sofa. "Yes," she went on, "where would we criminals be if they outlawed them?"

"In jail!" burst out Teasdale, and in a flash emerged head-first from the secrecy of the sofa and bit Mrs. Bell on the ankle with all his might. Mrs. Bell gave a shriek of pain and dropped the gun, and Jon was able to get to it before she could.

"They hurt Beth's ankle when we were in your office fighting," Teasdale told her, "now I've hurt yours with a little bit of biting!"

"Captured by a poet!" moaned Mrs. Bell as Beth, Leo, Aunt Henrietta, and Mrs. Fillipelli charged into the room.

We had to restrain Mrs. Fillipelli from leaping on Mrs. Bell, though nothing could restrain the angry tirade Mrs. Fillipelli delivered in Italian.

"Can it!" snapped Mrs. Bell. "My lawyer's here, and he'll get me off—you wait and see! You're going to need a lawyer when I accuse you of slander."

"We sure could use a lawyer!" agreed Leo.

"And a good one, too," added Beth. "Like our dad!"

131

"Did someone call for me?" said a familiar voice from behind us.

"Christopher Columbus!" cheered Beth. "Dad! What are you doing here?"

"I thought you knew—I'm the new board member from New York!" explained our dad as he entered the room.

"And don't neglect me!" pronounced a voice right behind him—and there was our own Granny Bea!

It was one big family reunion!

"Oh Dad! Oh Granny!" we cried as we raced to engulf them both in huge happy hugs!

Chapter Sixteen

Gatehouses and Good-byes

The police arrived soon after. They rounded up Bill, Frank, and Jasper, along with Mrs. Bell, and were loading them into a paddy wagon when Mrs. Bell made a mad dash for freedom.

Before the police even knew she was gone, she had leaped into her Toyota, thinking to drive it away. Too late she noticed the front end of the car looked more like an accordion than a car—thanks to Aunt Henrietta. The next thing we knew, Mrs. Fillipelli appeared by the side of the car, ripped open the door, and yanked Mrs. Bell out by her ear.

As Mrs. Fillipelli dragged Mrs. Bell by us toward the paddy wagon, our granny stepped forward to get a closer look.

"If it isn't Odelia Featherberry!" she snorted—then gave Mrs. Bell a ringing slap across the face.

"I've waited fifty years to give that old vulture what she deserves!" our granny informed us as Mrs. Fillipelli picked up Mrs. Bell and deposited her in the wagon.

Our granny explained that she and Mrs. Bell, formerly Miss Featherberry, had attended the same college a half century before—and that Mrs. Bell had been expelled for copying from our granny's final exam.

As the paddy wagon rattled out of the parking lot, we waved the criminals farewell.

"Have fun in jail!" called out Beth with great gusto.

"Send 'em on a one-way trip to outer space!" was Leo's parting piece of advice.

But it was Teasdale who summed it all up best by saying:

"Learn to be good or I promise that
   Mrs. Fillipelli will come and squash you flat!"

We left Hidden Mountain the next day. Every one of our
new friends came out to the parking lot to see us off. We
felt sad saying good-bye to Mrs. Fillipelli and Anna, though
we all planned a reunion at Hidden Mountain for the following summer.

We felt less sad saying good-bye to Mr. O'Hanrahan.

"I wish *I* were leaving!" he informed us. "This hotel is
simply not conducive to good writing—much too noisy!
Only yesterday evening, as I was trying to write in a small
room I found, not far from the kitchen—you know, the one
where the big freezer is; I doubt you've seen it—the most
annoying screams absolutely ruined my concentration!
Imagine someone making so much noise when *I* was trying
to write!"

"Perhaps someone was in real trouble," suggested Beth.

"Really, Beth!" replied Mr. O'Hanrahan and threw his
hands up in the air. "What a foolish notion! And anyway,
I was working on a most important scene—one that stressed
the worth of helping one's fellow man when he is in need!"

As we were packing up our dad's car, Jon raced over and
started shaking our dad's hand enthusiastically. "Thank you,
thank you!" he repeated.

Our dad then told us the board had voted to keep Hidden
Mountain open—and they had decided the one to run it
would be Jon! And of course they fired the members bribed
by Mrs. Bell and chose honest new ones to replace them.

Aunt Henrietta then joined in the good-bye-a-thon. She
had so fallen in love with the place, and felt so happy
there, that she'd asked Jon if she could stay on as social
director. Of course he'd said yes; in fact she still works
there today.

Jon also produced special trophies the hotel wanted to

give us, each with the word "Hero" engraved on it. As he was giving us these, a local newspaper reporter arrived, so an interview with us along with a big photo ended up being in the paper. And what's more, they even printed a poem by Teasdale in the same issue.

While the flashbulbs were flashing and the reporter was asking us questions, Beth noticed huge smiles on our dad's and our granny's faces. They were smiling at all of us, but especially at Teasdale and Henrietta. Beth knew this because she had overheard our granny telling our dad that Henrietta was a woman reborn—whatever that means.

As for Teasdale, even Leo noticed the change in him. I think he was prouder of his climb up the ladder than any of us really guessed, even though he did write eighty-seven poems about it afterward.

Even so, Beth had a few kind of sad thoughts about the whole adventure. She thinks money must be pretty terrible stuff sometimes if it can make people do such mean things to each other. Beth thinks it might take her a while to start trusting people again—she really thought Mrs. Bell and Bill were our friends. Henrietta says this is just a part of growing up, and these kinds of thoughts are balanced out by the good ones, and by good things happening—such as making new friends, like Jon, Anna, and Mrs. Fillipelli.

Pops Simon then showed up with candy canes for everyone, Mrs. Fillipelli gave a speech, Anna sang an old Russian folk song, there were more good-bye hugs and kisses, and finally we piled into our dad's car and drove off down the long Hidden Mountain driveway.

As we reached the main road, we stopped to point out to our dad and granny the little gatehouse which we'd so admired upon arriving. But it was gone. In its place was Aunt Henrietta's Panhard—and *under* the Panhard, all splinters and rubble, was the remains of the gatehouse.

"Christopher Columbus!" laughed Beth. "If we really wanted to punish Mrs. Bell, Jasper, Frank, and Bill, we'd cancel their jail terms and make them take a drive with Aunt Henrietta!"

Jon   Teasdale LEO Beth anna FILLY
      Henrietta